M000309270

Finding the # Dragon

(Stonefire Dragons #10)

Jessie Donovan

This book is a work of fiction. Names, characters, places, and incidents are either the product of the writer's imagination or are used fictitiously, and any resemblance to actual persons, living or dead, business establishments, events, or locales is entirely coincidental.

Finding the Dragon
Copyright © 2017 Laura Hoak-Kagey
Mythical Lake Press, LLC
First Print Edition

All rights reserved. This book or any portion thereof may not be reproduced or used in any manner without the express written permission of the author except for the use of brief quotations in a book review.

Cover Art by Clarissa Yeo of Yocla Designs
ISBN: 978-1942211570

Other Books by Jessie Donovan

<u>Stonefire Dragons</u>
Sacrificed to the Dragon
Seducing the Dragon
Revealing the Dragons
Healed by the Dragon
Reawakening the Dragon
Loved by the Dragon
Surrendering to the Dragon
Cured by the Dragon
Aiding the Dragon
Finding the Dragon
Craved by the Dragon (March 2018)

<u>Lochguard Highland Dragons</u>
The Dragon's Dilemma
The Dragon Guardian
The Dragon's Heart
The Dragon Warrior

<u>Kelderan Runic Warriors</u>
The Conquest
The Barren
The Heir (Jan 2018)

<u>Asylums for Magical Threats</u>
Blaze of Secrets
Frozen Desires
Shadow of Temptation
Flare of Promise

<u>Cascade Shifters</u>
Convincing the Cougar
Reclaiming the Wolf
Cougar's First Christmas
Resisting the Cougar

CHAPTER ONE

*J*ane Hartley watched the progress bar on the computer screen as her first videocast episode uploaded. After months of preparation and waiting, she was finally getting to start her new career. *The Dragon-shifter Insider* would not only be a contribution to helping her clan, but she also hoped that it would further develop relations and understanding between humans and dragon-shifters in the UK and beyond.

If only it would bloody upload faster. Even though she should wait weeks to truly gauge how it was received, she yearned for feedback sooner. She wouldn't be able to get any until the blasted thing was live, though.

Her mate, Kai Sutherland, stood behind her and squeezed her shoulders. "Staring at the screen won't make it work faster."

She frowned up at him. Sometimes it was irritating how much her mate knew her. "Trying to make it upload faster is only part of it."

He raised an eyebrow. "So if you're only 99 percent trying to make it work faster, what's the remaining percent?"

With anyone else, she might feel foolish sharing her thoughts. But not with Kai. "I'm also trying to memorize this moment."

"Why? I would think people watching and commenting

would be more memorable."

Leaning her head against his belly behind her, she sighed. "Every once in a while I wish you'd be more supportive instead of truthful."

The corner of his mouth ticked up. "Supportive has a time and a place. However, being honest pushes us to be better, as I believe you always say."

Jane stuck out her tongue. "So you were listening."

"I always listen, Janey." Kai lowered his head, his voice gravelly as he said, "That way I know the best ways to please you."

She shivered at his husky voice. "How you can still have this effect on me after all these months, I'll never know. You must have some sort of dragon-shifter magic you haven't told me about."

He moved to her side and tugged her up against him. "Not magic, love. You're mine, and I will always want you. It's my duty to make each time seem like the first, or maybe even better than the first. The second my female has a complaint, it's a sign that I'm not being a proper mate."

She looped her arms around his neck. "And to think the clan says you're unromantic."

Kai grunted. "You have your own sort of magic, I think. I say things to you that I'd never say otherwise."

"It's not magic, Kai. It's love." She searched his eyes. "And I hope it's enough."

"Of course it is. You're mine, Janey. And I pity the human or dragon who ever tries to take you away from me."

She couldn't resist poking her dragonman. "So, my love is enough even when I sneak off to shoot a new episode without telling you?"

He searched her eyes. "You didn't do that again, did you? I can't keep making exceptions for you, Jane. Of course I love you, but I can't allow the clan rules to break down."

"I only broke the rules once in recent months. Besides, the clan lockdown was to protect against a threat to dragon-shifters, so it technically didn't apply to me."

There had been a temporary ban on leaving the clan's lands after a recent attack, which had affected a few dragon-shifters via special drug darts. During that time, Jane had snuck off to interview someone from the Scottish clan, Lochguard, for her new series.

Kai replied, "Just because the drones we found had harmful chemicals for dragon-shifters doesn't mean there aren't ones for humans as well. After all, Stonefire seems to attract humans like flies to honey."

Clan Stonefire was her home, located in the Lake District in the North of England.

She kissed him gently before murmuring, "But humans coming to Stonefire has not only brought many more babies to the clan, but also allies for our leader."

As soon as she mentioned babies, Jane regretted it. Kai's mother asked every time they talked if she had any grandchildren on the way. And as much as Jane wished to grant the dragonwoman's request, she wasn't ready. After all, she'd been with Kai less than a year. Between his secret security operations and her reporting, there wasn't time for midnight feedings and living on two hours of sleep.

And yet, Kai's mother, Lily Owens, had been nothing but kind and supportive since the beginning. Jane wished there was a solution to make everyone happy.

Kai placed a possessive hand on her arse. "Stop fretting, Janey. Mum will be happy when the time is right. You are bloody amazing at what you do, and everyone on Stonefire appreciates you putting your life on the line for them. Again."

"Even you?"

He grunted. "As much as I can, given how my dragon bangs on about your safety."

She smiled. "I know how to calm him. Do both of you need some dragon cuddles?"

"No bloody dragon cuddles. Why can't you call it 'dragon loving' or 'dragon affection.' Both are more acceptable for a head Protector's mate."

Kai was in charge of Stonefire's security team, or Protectors, as the dragons called them.

Laughing, she snuggled against Kai's chest. "Because I like to rile you up every once in a while. You're stoic and calm for the clan's sake. But even a big, bad Protector needs to let go every once in a while."

He lightly slapped her arse. "How long will your uploading take?"

She raised her head again. "Not very long. Why?"

Kai's pupils flashed to slits. "Because my dragon and I want to do our own brand of cuddling."

As Kai's hand moved further down her bum and to between her thighs, heat flushed her cheeks. "I thought you had your fill this morning."

He pressed against the seam of her jeans and Jane sucked in a breath. Kai's hot breath tickled her ear as he whispered, "I will never have my fill of you, Jane Hartley. You're mine, and I think it's time to show you once more just how much I love you."

Instead of sitting in front of the computer, hitting Refresh every minute to see any comments, she would much prefer Kai naked and inside her.

Not that she'd surrender so easily.

She tilted her head. "Does that mean your dragon is going to come out to play?"

"I want you all to myself."

"And you've been doing so for over a week. I'd rather

he come out some of the time instead of waking up to find him in charge. Once he finishes, I can never muster the strength to get out of bed."

Concern filled Kai's eyes. "I told him you're merely a human."

She cupped his cheek. "I'm strong, Kai, and I love both halves of you. However, you would be the same way if you were shoved to the side for a week and could only watch, but never touch. The two of you make a whole, and I love you as you are. It's okay to share with him. After all, I plan to stick around for a long time to come. There's more than enough time for you and your dragon to have some fun."

"You'd better stick around."

She smiled. "Are you going to suggest your stubbornness can keep me alive forever?"

"Maybe."

She chuckled. "I'm not going anywhere, so stop worrying. I'd rather you use the energy for something else."

Kai's blue eyes with a ring of green around his pupils turned heated. "Then I had better start diverting that energy now."

Before she could do more than open her mouth, Kai tossed her over his shoulder and headed up the stairs. "Kai, what are you doing?"

He patted her bum. "This way is faster."

"You always say that," she muttered.

"Then stop asking and use the energy for something else."

Touché.

Not that Jane had time to think of a comeback. Within seconds, Kai had gently laid her down on their bed and moved away to shuck his clothes.

Even though she had licked every inch of Kai's body many times over, her mouth went dry at the sight of his muscled, naked chest. When he dropped his trousers, his hard cock sprung free. "Commando again, I see."

He took his cock in hand and stroked once. "I know you like me naked quicker."

She licked her lips. "Yes, I do."

And Jane also knew that if she didn't undress, she would lose yet another set of clothes to Kai's talons.

Somehow she forced her gaze away from Kai stroking his dick to quickly pull off her top and jeans. She'd also gone sans underwear.

He growled. "And to think I could've merely bent you over the chair, tugged your jeans down, and taken you downstairs."

Winking, Jane murmured, "I like to keep you guessing." She slowly opened her legs. "But enough talking. I'm waiting, dragonman. Come and take me."

Without another word, Kai covered her body with his. Positioning his dick, he rubbed up and down her wet folds before thrusting inside her. Jane gripped onto Kai's shoulders as he began to move.

⌀⌀⌀⌀

Kai tried to focus on his naked female's needs, but his bloody dragon kept growling and pacing inside his head. His beast spoke up once more. *I want her, too.*

You've done enough. Today is a big day and I don't want you exhausting her.

I wouldn't have to do marathon sex sessions if you shared.

Jane raked her nails down his back, and he met her blue-eyed gaze. "It's okay, Kai. I can handle your dragon."

See? She wants me.

For a split second, Kai hesitated. He loved his beast,

but every day he wondered if Kai or his dragon would do something to drive her away.

His beast huffed. *Stop it. She will stay.*

After another few pumps of his hips, Kai replied, *Just don't hurt her.*

NEVER.

With a roar, his beast took control of Kai's body and brain.

He watched as his dragon lifted Jane's legs and increased his pace. Jane clung to his shoulders as her breasts bounced. She moaned before saying, "Yes, right there."

Releasing one of her legs, his beast lightly flicked the bundle of nerves between her thighs. The pressure built at their spine, but even his impatient dragon gritted their teeth and held back.

Jane would come first in all ways.

When she finally screamed his name and gripped his cock, his dragon let go. Pleasure coursed through his body as he came.

After spending the last drop, his beast murmured, "Mine, Janey. Love you."

She traced his cheek. "I love both of you."

His dragon said to him, *Thank you. Take care of her. Always.*

Kai took control of his mind again and moved so that he was on his back with Jane on his chest. For a few beats, he merely listened to her thundering heart and reveled in her skin against his.

He was content to cuddle his mate in silence, but Jane's voice filled the room. "I wish you wouldn't worry so much, Kai." She paused and added, "I'm stronger than you think."

Looking down at his mate, he wanted to slap himself for the hurt he saw in her eyes. "You're one of the strongest humans I've ever met. But I can't help worrying."

She finished his thought. "I'm not *her*, Kai. I won't leave you."

"Her" referred to Maggie Jones, his true mate who had been so afraid of him that she'd run and mated another over a decade ago.

His dragon growled. *Why do you bring* her *up? She is not worth our time. Jane is better than that female.*

Rationally, I know that. But Jane and I are both stubborn and headstrong. She may tire of always challenging and fighting with me.

Jane's voice prevented his dragon from replying. "Tell me what you're saying to your dragon. You know you can tell me anything."

He took a section of her dark hair between his fingers and rubbed the soft strands. "It's not easy, Janey. You deserve a strong, confident mate."

"Kai, you are a strong, confident mate. Everyone has their worries. I worry about cheating your mother and mine out of a grandchild, or if my new series will end up hurting the dragon-shifters more than helping them. Hell, I sometimes wish I wasn't so curious and determined because I know it ends up causing you headaches. But I can't change everything about me just because I want to. I work on some things and accept others. You need to do the same."

His dragon grunted. *She is fantastic.*

Kai ignored his beast to gently kiss his female. "I'll try. I do love you, Jane Hartley, headaches and all."

She smiled. "Good, because I may have one or two other minor headaches I need to tell you about."

Before he could ask what they were, Kai's mobile phone rang. Since the ringtone was the one assigned to Bram, Stonefire's clan leader, Kai needed to take it.

Kissing Jane one last time, he moved from the bed to his clothes on the floor. He plucked his mobile from his trouser pocket and answered it. "Bram?"

"Aye, it's me. Sorry to interrupt you on Jane's big day, but something's happened."

"Just tell me straight, Bram."

His clan leader hesitated a second. Bram never hesitated. The news wasn't good.

Bram finally said, "It has to do with your sister, Delia. Come to my cottage as quickly as you can and I'll tell you everything."

Delia was Kai's much younger half sister, who lived in Wales on Clan Snowridge with his mother and stepfather.

Once Bram hung up, Kai lowered his phone and stared at it. He was confident that if Delia were dead, Bram would've said so. His clan leader was most definitely not a coward.

Kai should be relieved at that fact, but there were worse things a sixteen-year-old dragon-shifter could get up to than death.

Stop worrying and let's visit Bram. Only once we know what's wrong can we think of a plan, his dragon stated.

Jane asked, "What's wrong?"

He met his female's gaze. "Get dressed. Something's happened to Delia and we need to see Bram."

15

CHAPTER TWO

Fifteen minutes later, Jane tightened her grip on Kai's hand as they entered Bram's home office. Her dragonman might seem unaffected on the outside, but she knew how much he cared for his sister. Especially since he'd wasted so many years avoiding the Welsh clan, Snowridge, which in turn meant avoiding his family.

After all, Maggie Jones still lived on Snowridge.

Jane had never seen more than a glimpse of the dragonwoman during her previous visits. At some point, she'd like to meet the woman who had caused so much pain to Kai, more out of curiosity than anything else.

Well, and to let the woman know she'd had her chance and she had better not try to ruin Kai's life again.

As Bram motioned for them to sit down, Jane pushed all thoughts of Maggie out of her mind to focus on her clan leader's words. "I'll be blunt, Kai. Delia's missing."

Kai frowned. "Missing? For how long?"

"A few days, although your mother received a voice mail message last night from Delia, saying she was safe. And before you demand why you haven't been told, I didn't know myself until right before I called you. Snowridge's leader, Rhydian, had wanted to try locating her on his own. Your mother had been forbidden to ask for outside help."

Kai growled. "I'm not just any outsider. She's my little sister, for fuck's sake."

"Believe me, I know. But let's focus on the facts, aye? Delia originally left a brief note for her parents saying she had a story she wanted to investigate."

Jane stilled. Delia had interrogated her at every opportunity about being a journalist. She had never imagined the teenager would go off on her own.

As if reading her thoughts, Kai squeezed her hand in reassurance. He didn't blame her.

Kai probed. "About what?"

Bram shook his head. "That's unclear. The notes that were forwarded to me are somewhat vague and unhelpful. Her message yesterday merely said that she was okay and not to worry."

"Did they trace the call?" Kai asked.

"Aye, it was from a pay phone in a remote part of Wales. Snowridge's Protectors have been searching, but your sister hasn't been spotted anywhere. You didn't teach her how to hide in plain sight, did you?"

"Of course not. Although I might be able to find her, even if the others can't," Kai replied.

Bram bobbed his head. "I know, which is why I've managed to negotiate a deal with Snowridge's leader. He's going to allow you to go to Snowridge and help search for Delia."

Jane jumped in. "You said negotiate. In exchange for what?"

"That's my concern, lass. Right now, the end goal is to find Delia," Bram stated.

"When can I go?" Kai asked.

"As soon as you have everything set up for your absence. With Aaron recently mated to Teagan O'Shea, it leaves a bit of a gap in the chain of command."

Aaron Caruso had been Kai's second-in-command of the Stonefire Protectors. However, Aaron had gone to strengthen alliances with a clan in Ireland and had ended up mating their female leader, Teagan O'Shea.

Kai nodded. "That may be, but I think Nikki can handle the clan whilst I'm gone."

Amusement danced in Bram's eyes. "Make sure her mate is on board with that."

Nikki Gray's mate was Jane's older brother, Rafe. Ever since Nikki had become pregnant, he'd become even more overprotective.

Jane was just glad she wasn't on the receiving end of it.

She waved a hand. "Leave Rafe to me. I'll convince him right quick and then we can leave."

Kai looked at her. "We?"

"If you think I'm going to stay behind, you're out of your mind. I can help, Kai. Putting together clues and finding people is a big part of my life."

Bram stepped in. "She's right. Besides, Rhydian cleared the pair of you since you've both been to Snowridge several times already. I'd say he almost trusts you, which is a rare thing with that bastard." He stood. "Go see Nikki and Rafe and be on your way. Make sure to keep me updated on Delia's status, as well as your own."

Kai stood and tugged Jane up with him. Her dragon-man grunted before guiding her out of Bram's house.

Her mate remained silent until they were far enough away from Bram's cottage so as to not be overheard. She wondered if he had it down to the inch as he finally said, "If you're coming with me, then you need to promise me you won't go off anywhere without telling me. I usually don't try to curb your freedom too much, but Snowridge is unfamiliar territory, complete with humans who don't trust the dragons as much as those near Stonefire. I can't risk losing you, Janey. I won't survive it."

Any retort she had died at his last sentence. "I'm not a wilting flower, but I'll be careful. However, if something comes up that requires immediate action or we might lose your sister, I will seize the opportunity. I have no wish to die, but I'm not about to let your sister come to harm, either."

He threaded his fingers of one hand through her hair. "You're noble for a human."

She raised her brows. "I'm not noble, just stubborn. I won't allow any more pain in your life if I can help it. Your sister is important to you, which means she's important to me."

⌒⌒⌒⌒

Jane Hartley was the best bloody female he could've ever hoped for. Not for the first time, he mentally gave the finger to fate for thinking anyone else would've suited him.

His beast hummed. *Jane is our perfect fit. I agree.*

As Kai took in his mate's straightened shoulders and raised chin, pride surged through his body. "You are worthy of being a head Protector's mate."

The corner of her mouth ticked up. "Even though I like to give dragon cuddles?"

He chuckled. "Yes, despite that." Moving his hand from her hair to her cheek, he added, "Just be careful, Janey. You are strong, confident, and clever, but you're human. It's not a bad thing, I rather love you for it, but you don't heal as fast as a dragon-shifter, nor do you have the option to shift to better protect yourself."

She nodded. "I know, but I like to think I've come a long way from going undercover in that pub in Newcastle."

Jane had worn a tight dress, too much makeup, and a

wig. She'd gone into a pub to try to win the trust of some dragon hunters. The incident had ended with Kai being shot and both of them being flown back to Stonefire gripped in Nikki's talons.

Never again did he want to see a worthless piece-of-shit hunter putting a hand on his female.

His dragon spoke up. *Let them try. They'll learn their lesson soon enough.*

Ignoring his beast, Kai pulled Jane up against his body. "You're maybe a tad bit better." He kissed her ear. "But don't ever completely change who you are for anyone, Jane, not even me."

She gave him a quick kiss. "Good, because I'm going to need all of this backbone and stubbornness to deal with my brother."

"Your bloody brother," Kai muttered.

"Oh, you like him well enough when you two team up against me."

Kai grunted. "Sometimes. Let's go tell Nikki the news. I'll draw her into another room once I announce, then you can deal with Rafe. Nikki doesn't need the stress of another row."

Jane rolled her eyes. "I'm going to resist commenting on that."

His dragon spoke up. *Coward.*

I'm not a coward. It's a matter of efficiency to divide up the tasks.

Tell yourself that. At least we know Delia should still be safe since she left a message yesterday.

Let's hope so. If something had been wrong, Mum would've heard it in Delia's voice.

His beast stood tall inside his mind. *Don't worry, we're better than the Welsh Protectors. They probably overlooked something. We'll find her.*

He took comfort from his beast's words. *I won't stop until we do.*

His dragon fell silent, and Kai took comfort from Jane's presence. He patted his mate's arse. "Good. Then let's go. The sooner we talk to Nikki, the sooner we can leave."

Despite the hurry, Kai kept his arm around Jane's waist as they walked briskly to Nikki and Rafe's cottage. Since his rather tall human was only two inches shorter than him, she didn't struggle to keep up.

As they made their way, he remembered something. With everything Bram had told him, Kai had temporarily forgotten about Jane's big launch. "I'm sorry we had to ruin your big day, Janey. I hope any new viewers will understand you missing the scheduled Q&A session this evening."

She smiled up at him. "It's okay. Gina will post an announcement."

Gina MacDonald-MacKenzie was mated to a Scottish dragon-shifter and had been helping Jane with marketing and publicity. "So you had a backup plan in place?"

"Of course. Given how much Stonefire is a target these days, I had to be prepared."

"My clever mate."

She shrugged. "A certain male dragon-shifter likes to say how much preparation is key to success."

He couldn't help but murmur, "So you were listening."

Jane snorted and lightly slapped his side. "That is a conversation we can have later." Her face sobered. "As much as I look forward to this new chapter in my life, the strangers can wait. Delia is family. Besides, while I'd never wish for your sister to be in harm's way, this mission will at least keep me distracted."

"Mission, huh?"

"Of course. We should think of a secret code name."

"Dragons don't usually give code names."

"Well, seeing as I'm human, that means I can." She tapped her chin, and he couldn't help but smile at the action. Jane finally added, "How about Operation Teenage Rebellion?"

"More like Operation Bloody Idiot."

Jane laughed. "See, I knew I could get you on board."

He smiled at Jane's laugh and realized his mate had been trying to calm him down and distract him from his sister's disappearance. "Thanks, Janey. Maybe now I won't kill your brother."

"Not killing Rafe is one of the unbreakable rules of our relationship." She lowered her voice. "Although if he's too much of a bastard, feel free to punch him. That's allowed on rare occasions."

Kai shook his head as they arrived at Nikki and Rafe's cottage. He knocked and Nikki opened the door. "Kai, I didn't expect to see you today."

Rafe's voice drifted from inside the cottage. "What the bloody hell does he want now? We're busy."

Nikki grinned. "Don't mind him. If he had it his way, we'd always be 'busy.'"

Kai took in Nikki's mussed hair and rumpled shirt. "I'm going to pretend I didn't notice that. This is important, Nikki. Let us in."

At Kai's serious tone, Nikki stepped aside and they walked into the cottage. Once she closed the door, she looked between him and Jane. "What happened?"

Rafe appeared at Nikki's side as Kai explained his sister's situation and added, "Which means I need you to be in charge in my absence."

Nikki blinked. "Me? Are you sure?"

"You have the most experience when it comes to the hunters and even the Dragon Knights. Not only that, you've proven yourself over and over again." Rafe opened his mouth, but Kai spoke first. "And before you bring up her pregnancy for the hundredth time this week, Nikki will be fine. She's months away from giving birth and I trust her to delegate as needed."

Rafe grunted. "I still don't like it. Nikki doesn't need the stress. Dr. Sid said she needed to take it easy."

Jane chimed in. "Easy doesn't mean putting her in a bed and wrapping her in blankets to prevent the slightest bump. Am I right, Nikki?"

Nikki looked to her mate. "I'll be fine, Rafe." She met Kai's gaze. "Although I want Rafe to be my right-hand man. He's still waiting for the specifics of his army liaison post and needs a purpose."

"I have a purpose," Rafe replied. "It's protecting you and our child."

Kai squeezed Jane's side, signaling for her to take Rafe in hand. Once Jane nodded, Kai said, "Nikki, come with me and we'll discuss everything, including your mate's temporary role."

Rafe stepped in front of Nikki. "We still need to hash out the details of her post, and I want to be present for that."

Jane poked her brother's arm. "Just stop, Rafe. Nikki can handle herself. Because I guarantee if you keep tiptoe-ing around her and treating her as if she'll shatter, she's going to hate you."

Rafe blinked. "She wouldn't."

Nikki smiled. "I may. So, go chat with Jane. I've important stuff to do."

Before Rafe could say anything else, Nikki waltzed out of the room, and Kai followed.

Once they were inside the kitchen, Kai muttered, "I'm not sure how you put up with him."

Nikki rolled her eyes. "I'd say the same of Jane with you. But enough about mates. Tell me what needs doing in your absence and I'll make sure it's done."

As Kai went through the current status of clan affairs and secret operations, he tried his best to ignore the shouting from the other room. After all, if anyone could handle Rafe Hartley outside of Nikki, it was Jane.

⌒﹋⌒﹋⌒﹋⌒

Jane glared at her brother. "Why do you insist on making everyone's life so bloody difficult?"

Rafe shrugged a shoulder. "There's nothing wrong with wanting to protect Nikki and our baby."

"What, so you're going to make me a villain for telling you to grow the fuck up?"

"If you were pregnant, you'd understand what I'm feeling, Janey."

"So now I need to be growing a child to understand wanting to protect someone?" She moved closer to Rafe and whispered, "Every time I go to Snowridge, I wonder if that woman will show up and cause Kai pain. Believe me, I know the feeling. But keeping him here just in case, to never risk the chance, would eventually tear me and him apart." She moved back to meet her brother's eyes. "Nikki is patient, and she loves you, but keep it up, and you might do something irreversible."

She expected Rafe to give her the double finger salute and tell her to mind her own fucking business. However, he merely sighed. "I know. But you of all people know how taking a step back is hard for me."

Jane resisted blinking at her brother's honesty. Maybe Nikki was having more of an influence on Rafe than Jane had given her credit for. "Then use this as an opportunity, Rafe. Help her, but don't smother her. Nikki may end up being the next second-in-command of the Protectors, which is a big deal. I don't think Stonefire's ever had a female in that position before."

"I don't think so either." He paused before adding, "I'll try and sorry for shouting. Your mate has a way of winding me up."

Jane snorted. "As I keep telling you, you and Kai act like brothers. Just embrace it and you'll have fewer headaches."

He raised his brows. "Have you told Kai the same?"

She shrugged. "That's for me to know and for you to wonder about."

"Janey," Rafe growled.

She ignored his warning tone. "On a more serious note, keep your mobile close. I may need help from your army contacts in locating Delia."

Rafe sobered. "I will. Regardless of what I think of Kai at times, I hope you find his sister."

"Me, too, Rafe. Me, too." She opened her arms. "Now, give your sister a hug."

He eyed her open arms. "British soldiers don't give hugs."

"Half-Australian brothers do." She engulfed him before he could move away.

After a few seconds, she released him. "Now, was that so bad?"

"It was fucking awful."

Patting his arm, she half-turned toward the hall to the kitchen. "Good. Now, let's see if they're nearly done with their meeting. I'm anxious to go."

CHAPTER THREE

*S*everal hours later, Kai flapped his wings as he maneuvered through the mountains on the outskirts of Snowridge's lands in Wales.

He glanced down at Jane, huddled in her blankets, and determined she was well enough. While his mate would occasionally stand up in the basket he gripped with his rear talons, she still wasn't fond of flying and spent most of the trip with her eyes closed.

His beast spoke up. *Look how far she's come in less than a year. Give it time. Maybe one day we can even rig a harness on our back and she can truly feel the wind and experience the freedom of the skies.*

So now we're to be ridden like a horse?

His dragon huffed. *Why do you like to ruin my beautiful dreams? Allowing anyone to ride on a dragon's back is an honor and the highest sign of trust. Unless you're saying you don't trust Jane?*

Don't be stupid, of course I trust her. But she's not fond of unstable heights. Have some compassion. Riding on our back will give her a fucking heart attack.

When his beast didn't reply, Kai knew he'd won the point.

Slowing his wings, Kai mostly glided the remaining distance to Snowridge's main landing area. Unlike Stonefire, which was spread out on mostly flat land, the majority of Clan Snowridge lived inside the mountains near Snowdonia National Park in Northern Wales. The main landing area was one of the few flat, outdoor spaces that had been carved out many years ago.

Since he'd brought Jane to Snowridge many times in the past, he easily guided both him and the basket to the landing area without hitting any of the jutting, sharp edges. Once he gently placed the basket on the ground, he moved a few feet away and landed.

Kai imagined his wings shrinking into his back, his talons turning into fingers, and his snout returning to a human nose.

Once he was in his human form, Jane rushed at him and handed him his clothes. Kai quickly dressed.

Just as he tugged on his jumper, his mother's form appeared. Even though Lily Owens had the same blonde hair mixed with gray and a smile on her face as always, he could also see the strain of worry at the corner of her eyes and in her slightly hunched posture.

Jane rushed up to his mother and hugged her. "We'll find her, Lily. I promise."

His mother hugged back and released her. "I know." She looked to Kai. "Rhydian is waiting to see you, Kai. Unless you need a quick rest beforehand?"

Under normal circumstances, Kai would tell his mother that he wasn't a child. But until he found Delia, he would make an effort to be nicer. "I'm fine, Mum."

"Good. Then Jane can come with me whilst you talk with Rhydian."

Kai grunted. "No. Jane comes with me."

"After all this time, you can spare her a few minutes, Kai Wilbur Sutherland," Lily stated.

Jane spoke up. "It's not that, Lily. I'd love to sit down

with tea and biscuits and chat with you, but I'm here to help Kai find Delia. If I go with him now, then it'll save us a lot of time later."

Lily frowned at him. "Why didn't you just say that? Sometimes, I wish you'd be a little more chatty."

From the sides of his eyes, Kai noticed that Jane bit her lip to keep from smiling. He ignored his mate to focus on his mum. "So you've said many times before. However, Delia is our focus for the moment. Where's Rhydian now?"

Lily motioned toward the entrance into the mountain. "In his office. Since you've never set foot there before, I'll take you."

In the next instant, Lily turned her head away and raised a hand to her face. *Shit.* He only hoped his strong, cheerful mum wasn't crying.

Maybe she and Rhydian had played down the danger to Delia.

He glanced at Jane, and she motioned with her head at his mother.

His beast spoke up. *She wants us to lend support. It won't kill you to hug her.*

I sometimes wonder how you were ever paired with me.

You're just lucky.

Resisting a sigh, Kai went to his mother's side and put an arm around her shoulders. He was a good six inches taller, so he kissed the top of her head. "I'll find her, Mum. I vow it."

Lily sniffed. "I know you will, Kai. But it's hard not knowing if she's all right or if her call was forced. I didn't hear fear or nervousness, but it was a short message, and sometimes even the best mother can be fooled by a teenager."

Jane jumped in. "Don't be so hard on yourself, Lily. I'm

positive that Kai inherited his ability to detect liars and deceivers from you. Not even a determined teenage daughter should be able to fool you." Jane took a step toward the mountain's entrance. "Now, how about we see your clan leader? The sooner we have information, the faster we can find Delia."

His mum murmured her assent and finally started walking.

As Lily guided them into one of the mountain passages and down a corridor carved into the rock, Kai did his best to support his mother. He'd been a horrible son for so many years, avoiding her in order to protect his heart from Maggie. The least he could do was find Delia and bring her back safely. It would go a long way toward making up for his neglect.

Although once he found his sister, Kai would hug her once and then give a rather long, stern lecture about common sense and using it.

His beast snorted. *As if that will work. It didn't work with us, either, at her age.*

It doesn't mean I won't try. After all, I know what sort of trouble she could get into.

Rather than answer, his dragon merely shook his head.

His mother made one last turn and stopped in front of an old, wide door made of wood and metal. She knocked, and Kai did his best to pack away his dislike of the Snowridge leader. Their meetings had been few, but the male had never been friendly or warm like Bram. He also had a tendency to share the bare minimum.

In other words, Kai had his work cut out for him.

⁘

As Kai knocked on the old, wooden door, Jane mentally

prepared herself for her first formal meeting with Rhydian Griffiths. Sure, she'd met him for a few seconds here and there, but he seemed not to care much for humans in general.

After all, Jane hadn't been able to find any recent cases of human sacrifices on Snowridge or dragon-shifters finding their true mates in humans and bringing them back to the Welsh clan.

The only semi-related case she knew about was the half-human and half-dragon-shifter child of Gwendolen Price. The father of her child, Noah Tucker, had been human and Rafe's best mate for a long time. Unfortunately, Noah had died saving a pregnant Gwen during their time in the British Army. The tragedy was probably why Rhydian had welcomed the half-human child into his clan.

Or, maybe Jane was being harsher than was fair. The meeting should allow her to form a more accurate idea of the dragonman. Being leader was never easy, and while she wished everyone had a sense of humor and understanding like Bram or even Finn Stewart on Lochguard, leaders had to act according to their clan's needs.

The door opened and Jane focused on the man standing in the doorway. Rhydian was in his forties with jet-black hair and blue eyes. The set of three scars on one cheek gave him an edgy appearance. No matter how hard she'd tried, she hadn't been able to wheedle out how he'd received them in the first place. Jane thought they were from him being slashed by dragon talons.

Rhydian nodded at Kai and then glanced at Jane. "Why is the human here? She's allowed on my land, but I want to talk with you alone, Kai."

Kai shook his head. "No. Jane's here to help and has every right to hear what you're going to say."

Rhydian stared at Jane with his assessing eyes, but she

merely raised an eyebrow. "If you know Kai at all, then you know I'm immune to such stares. Glares and growls as well, I might add."

For a second, Snowridge's leader remained silent, and Jane wondered if she'd overstepped a line. Then he nodded toward the inside of the room. "Then the pair of you come inside. Lily, you've heard this before, so maybe you should go back to Gareth."

Gareth was Lily's mate and Kai's stepfather.

Lily touched Kai's arm. "Come find me when you're done."

Once the dragonwoman was out of sight, Rhydian stepped aside. Jane and Kai entered the room.

As soon as Rhydian shut the door, he turned to face them. "I've spared your mother some of the details, Kai, but in the last few hours, some of my Protectors might have discovered where Delia went."

"Where?" Kai demanded.

Not for the first time, Jane loved how Kai could focus on what's important rather than dwell on details, such as the fact Rhydian had kept information from Lily.

The Welsh leader moved to his desk and sat on the edge. He picked up a file folder and held it out. "Everything we know is in here, but the short of it is some of the dragon-shifter children from the local farms have gone missing. I think Delia has been trying to find them."

Kai took the folder but never broke his gaze with Rhydian. "What the bloody hell are you talking about?"

"Unlike on Stonefire, we can't farm on our land since it almost entirely consists of mountains and rock. The Welsh humans long ago gave us farming rights to nearby arable land, and we don't advertise it for obvious reasons. The farmers are careful to appear human whenever possible, to protect their identities. On top of that, Snowridge's Protectors do daily sweeps to ensure everything is okay."

Jane jumped in, "But something must've gone wrong."

"Correct, Ms. Hartley. Last week, one child went missing from one of the outermost farms. Then a few days later, a pair of siblings also disappeared on the opposite side of our farming area. At that point, I evacuated the farmers and brought them here until we could figure out who's doing this. However, despite around the clock searches, no one has been able to find the missing children, nor do we know who is exactly responsible."

Jane wanted to say it was either the dragon hunters or Dragon Knights, but she bit her tongue. After all, there could be a local enemy to Snowridge she had no idea about.

Kai jumped in. "Does the entire clan know about this?"

Rhydian shook his head. "No. My head Protector and I merely said that some of the farmers were staying with us for a short while to visit their families living here. All of the farmers were sworn to secrecy as to the true reason. However, since it's summer, I'm sure the presence of the farmers is raising a few eyebrows. The high growing season isn't the best time for a visit."

Jane tilted her head. "Is that how Delia figured out what was going on? Or is there something else that I'm missing?"

Rhydian moved his gaze to Jane and answered, "She left the same day the farmers first arrived, so it's unlikely she put the clues together so quickly. Delia is clever but still a child with few resources, let alone contacts to divulge information. She must've overheard something at the Protectors' central command. She's been volunteering there, helping with administrative duties."

Kai grunted. "I'll comment on the lack of discretion amongst your Protectors later. What, exactly, did she overhear?"

Rhydian's pupils flashed to slits for a second before returning to round. Instead of reminding Kai of his place, he waved toward the folder. "It's all in there, but some of the Protectors think the children were taken by local dragon hunters. We don't have a unified front here similar to the likes of Simon Bourne, but the DDA's presence is sparse at best in the north of Wales, and our current theory is that someone took advantage of that fact."

Simon Bourne was the head of the largest dragon hunter group in the UK and was currently based near Birmingham in England. He'd also caused Stonefire many a headache, and his hunters had even killed one of their Protectors in the past.

Jane took a step forward. "So, let me get this straight. You think Delia went searching for dragon hunters. And not only that, but hunters who kidnapped children, to probably keep them captive and harvest their blood at maturity?"

Dragon's blood could cure many illnesses, but it only became usable once a dragon was an adult.

"Yes," Rhydian answered. "But before you start cursing at her stupidity, her note suggested investigating only and reporting on what she finds. She's clever, and I believe she'll keep out of harm's way if possible."

"You have more bloody faith than I do, Rhydian," Kai growled out. "We've all been sixteen before, and being rational isn't the most important of priorities at that stage."

Raising an eyebrow, Rhydian replied, "Berating a teenager is a waste of time. I've invited you here to help at your mother's request. My condition for that information is that you report anything you find. The last thing I need is Lily losing both of her children and a daughter-in-law in one blow."

Jane jumped in before Kai's temper flared. "Of course we'll tell you everything. I think it's best if Kai and I borrow a conference room and comb through these files. We want to make sure we know everything before searching the area."

Rhydian nodded. "There's one across the hall from my office that you can use." He picked up a sticky note with a number written on it. "This is Wren's number. He and Eira worked with some of your fellow Protectors in Scotland not that long ago and know a little bit about your clan. They've volunteered to help and be your clan liaisons."

Jane bet they were also going to be her and Kai's babysitters.

She took the small piece of paper. "Thank you. Hopefully we'll find Delia and the missing children soon."

"Report everything to me and we'll get along fine."

Jane turned Kai toward the door. "Thank you."

They exited the room and tried the door opposite Rhydian's office. Thankfully it opened. The instant it closed, Kai growled, "He doesn't seem to have much faith in us."

Jane raised her brows. "Then we need to work extra hard to prove how good we are." She opened the folder and handed Kai half of the papers. "Work will help tame your temper." She leaned over and kissed him briefly. "Delia is all that matters right now, love. Let's get to work."

For a second, Kai did nothing. Then he kissed her cheek and sat down. Jane followed suit. It was time to do what she did best and read between the lines to find a lead most would overlook.

CHAPTER FOUR

hree hours later, Kai flew in his dragon form ahead of Eira and Wren. Their destination was Delia's last known location, a town called Dolgellau.

He and Jane had memorized as many facts as possible. But until they could see both the farms where the children had been taken from as well as where Delia had made her call the night before, the trail would remain cold.

His beast spoke up. *I could fly faster if you'd let me.*

We have Jane to consider.

He glanced down at his brave human, clutched in Kai's back talons. She'd volunteered to travel that way, despite her fear of unstable heights.

His dragon answered, *I still say a harness would've been easier.*

And taken up too much bloody time. This way, I can ensure she doesn't fall to her death. The shape of Cadair Idris, the mountain which loomed over the small town of Dolgellau, came into view. Kai added, *Now, focus on gently putting Jane on her feet and shifting back. There's not much time before the post office shuts and we need to talk to them.*

Delia's call had been traced to the town's post office.

Thankfully his dragon closed the remaining distance in silence. Just outside the town, his beast found a wide open space to land. When they were only a few feet from the ground, he hovered in place to release Jane. His mate stumbled a second but quickly regained her balance. She moved away, signaling for Kai to land.

His feet touched the grass and Kai folded his golden wings against his back. Everything shrank back into his human form.

Jane came to his side with a forced smile. Uncaring that the Welsh dragon-shifters were landing just behind them, he caressed Jane's cheek. "Are you all right, Janey?"

She shook her whole body. "That's not something I'd do every day, that's for certain. Still, I'm fine." She lowered her voice, even though the only ones nearby were the two Welsh dragon-shifters, who possessed supersensitive hearing and could understand it anyway. "It'll be easier for later, if we need to fly under the cover of darkness and sneak in somewhere."

The corner of his mouth ticked up. "I don't need darkness to sneak, as you put it."

"Once all of this is sorted, I'm going to bring that up again." She pressed his clothes against his chest. "Now, hurry and get dressed."

Kai quickly put on his top and trousers. By the time he turned toward the other dragon-shifters, Eira and Wren were already waiting for him. Taking Jane's hand, he closed the distance between him and the others.

Wren nodded at him. "So far, the humans are keeping their distance. But we should probably hide whilst Jane goes into town. The humans in this area are more used to dragons than other parts of North Wales because of us patrolling the nearby farms, but I wouldn't exactly say they love us."

Kai looked to Jane. "Remember your promise."

"I know, if I see anything suspicious or suspect I'm

being followed, then I'll meet at the rendezvous point near the river. And I'm only to ring you if I'm positive no one can listen in."

"Good. Then go before I change my mind," Kai murmured.

Jane sighed, but turned and walked briskly toward the town. If she kept up the pace, it should take her ten minutes to get there.

His dragon spoke up. *She'll be fine. Let's hurry to the river just in case she needs us. I'm not sure how the humans in this town will react if they find out Jane is mated to a dragon-shifter.*

I suspect they know, considering most of the town can see this area.

Being carried by dragonwing is one thing, being mated is another.

Not wanting to listen to his beast drone on about possible dangers to Jane, Kai looked to his fellow Protectors. "Let's split up and each take a different route to the river. While unlikely, we might find clues along the way."

The Welsh dragons murmured their assent. Kai motioned toward the northwest. "I'll go that way. Wren, you travel directly north and, Eira, take the northeast. Make sure you're at the meeting point in an hour."

As Kai started walking, he tried his best to focus on finding clues. If Jane could handle acting and fooling Tobias White—a dragon hunter and key member in the scandal surrounding the former Director of Dragon Affairs—she could certainly handle talking to a postal worker in rural Wales.

His beast spoke up. *Knowing Janey, she won't stop at the post office.*

Thanks, dragon, for giving me something else to worry about.

Unlike you, I like to think of all possible outcomes. We must protect our mate.

Not wanting to argue with his dragon, Kai ignored him and studied his surroundings. It was a long shot that any dragon hunters had come this way, let alone left behind tracks or other clues, but Kai wasn't about to dismiss it. After all, the hunters had caused more havoc on his clan than any other enemy in recent memory. Underestimating them was foolish.

⌘⌘⌘

As Jane walked down a street called Smithfield, she spotted the red and yellow sign that denoted all post offices in the UK.

She turned the corner of the gray stone building and walked inside the newsagents. Not unlike the town where her parents lived, the post office operated inside the small store. She walked past the aisles of food, crisps, and sweets until she came to the queue line for the post office counter. A woman in her fifties stood alone with a slightly bored expression on her face.

Jane went to the woman. She had debated trying out her Welsh accent but had decided against it. This far north there were a lot of Welsh speakers, and Jane didn't know much beyond a handful of words.

She took out her mobile and smiled at the older woman. "I'm sorry to bother you, but I was wondering if you had seen this young woman recently?"

Jane showed a recent picture of Delia smiling at the camera—a sixteen-year-old girl with short, brown hair and green eyes.

The woman glanced at it and back to Jane. "Why are you asking about her?"

Not wanting to prompt the woman to ask too much about the specifics, she replied, "She's my sister-in-law and she's missing. I'm trying to help my husband find her."

Looking down again, the worker frowned. "She seems familiar. A tall girl like her was here yesterday, although she had much lighter hair. She asked to use the phone and sounded like she was local. I don't usually allow it, but her mobile had died and telephone boxes are hard to find anymore."

If Delia had indeed listened to everything Jane had told her about past assignments, she wouldn't rule out Delia wearing a wig or coloring her hair. "Did you overhear anything she said whilst using the phone?"

"No, I went toward the back to give her some privacy. I turned around for a moment, but when I looked over my shoulder, she was gone. You can ask the cashier if he saw anything. Gwilym worked yesterday, too."

Jane could leave it there, but she wasn't about to wonder what-if later. "Did my sister-in-law say anything else? Or did she only come to use the phone?"

"Nothing else that I can remember. Many people come this way in the summer for the walks, especially with Cadair Idris right there, so I barely pay attention to the unfamiliar folk during the tourist season. I only remember about the phone because so few people ask that anymore. Sorry, love."

"No worries. Thanks so much for your help."

Jane gave a half wave and turned around. While knowing that Delia might be in a partial disguise was useful, she hoped the cashier had more information. True, they had yet to visit the dragon-shifter farms for clues, but Jane was impatient. Delia was part of her family now and she was anxious to find her.

The young man at the cash register was in his early twenties, with dark hair and eyes. He looked up from his mobile and Jane asked, "Hello, did you speak to this girl yesterday?" She flashed Delia's picture again. "She's my sister-in-law, and I'm trying to find her."

"Yeah, she was the tall, fit girl asking about those tattooed blokes."

"Tattooed blokes?" she echoed.

He nodded. "She said they stole her bag and she was trying to track them down. I thought it odd and asked about the police, but they weren't helping her, or something like that. The three men with the tattoos come in here every week or two for cigarettes and then usually around the corner to the off-license for booze."

Jane had noticed the liquor shop on her way to the post office earlier. "Did you tell her anything else about them? Her brother's worried about her, and if she went off to possibly catch the thieves by herself, I need to know as much as you can tell me before she gets into too much trouble."

The man shrugged. "There wasn't much more to tell. All three blokes were Welsh with tattoos on their forearms, but that's about all I remember. Wait, none of them had facial hair, either. I told her it was best to wait for the police to catch them."

Jane forced herself to smile warmly. "Thanks for your help. If you see her again, please call this number." Jane handed over a card. The number was to one of the disposable phones she used for investigations and kept stashed in different locations. She wasn't about to let anyone find her via her personal number.

As Jane exited the store and turned the corner, she debated going into the off-license and asking more questions.

But then she had an idea. The post office and newsagents had security cameras. She bet that even in Northern Wales they backed up security feed to an online storage service. Well, the post office should, at any rate. All she needed to do was contact Arabella MacLeod, a brilliant hacker who had helped Jane in the past. The dragonwoman lived in Scotland with her mate and children, but she had been born and raised on Stonefire. Everyone, including her and Kai, trusted Arabella.

Since images would do better than another description of Welsh blokes with tattoos, Jane made her way north toward the river. She had a feeling the men Delia had asked about were connected to the kidnappings, or at least Delia believed so. Why Delia hadn't kept her distance and shared what she knew to Clan Snowridge, Jane had no idea.

If Delia were tracking down the men herself, it could end badly.

Picking up her pace, she nearly ran to the rendezvous point.

Kai would never blame Jane if anything happened to Delia, but Jane would blame herself. She'd pegged the teenager as being mature for her age and had told her too much about her past jobs. She needed to make it right, or she would end up causing more pain in Kai's life.

Jane only hoped Delia hadn't been captured yet. Considering what had happened to Arabella as a teenager, when she'd been abused and set on fire by dragon hunters, Jane's imagination started to run wild.

⁂

Kai wove his way through the trees along the river as he paced and resisted looking at his phone again. "Arabella is taking a bloody long time to send me those images."

"It's been five minutes, Kai," Jane stated.

He looked up at his mate. Despite her attempt at a calm face, worry danced in her eyes. "This is the only lead we have so far."

"Well, I could ask more people in town about the tattooed blokes, if it comes to it. Maybe someone noticed their car or which direction they drove off to. Not to mention Eira and Wren are at the farms now, looking for more clues."

His beast spoke up. *Don't take it out on Jane. She had the idea to ask Arabella in the first place.*

I know, but since no one found anything else useful and the Snowridge Protectors still haven't found her, I'm starting to worry.

Jane touched his arm. "If it were a clan member and not Delia, you'd be calmer. I know it's difficult, but everyone needs Protector Kai right now. Do you think he can make an appearance?"

"Can't I be both?"

She smiled at his growly tone. "What would everyone else think of Stonefire's head Protector sulking?"

"I'm not sulking. I'm worried and impatient. There's a difference."

Jane placed a hand on his chest. "If you say so."

His beast laughed. *You are acting like a child.*

Don't start. Besides, it's only Jane. She loves all of us.

Good thing, too. Without her in our lives, you'd probably have knocked a few heads together already and caused a ruckus.

Before he could reply, his phone buzzed. Taking it out, he opened it. Once he saw the caller ID, he put it on speakerphone. "What did you find, Arabella?"

Finlay Stewart, the Scottish dragon clan leader and Arabella's mate, growled. "Be nicer to Ara. After all, she did this despite having three wee bairns to look after."

Kai was about to tell him to fuck off, but Arabella's voice came over the line. "Ignore Finn. His amount of charm seems to correlate to how much sleep he has, and he hasn't had much of late."

"Not all of us are like you and can function well on three hours of sleep," Finn murmured.

Arabella carried on as if she hadn't heard her mate. "I did find the images, but they're unclear and pixelated. I'm having Ian and Emma work on cleaning them up, but I'll send the original ones for now."

Kai didn't know who Ian and Emma were, but didn't think it was important enough to ask. "Are you running the images against any databases you can access?"

"Of course, but it takes time, Kai. Just look at the pictures and deduce what you can yourself. I just wanted to let you know more is coming, because otherwise, I know you'd call up and demand something."

Jane spoke up. "I'll try to keep him in line, Arabella. Thanks for your help."

"Good luck," Arabella answered and she hung up.

Kai checked his email and opened the images. He made sure Jane could see them, too.

They were blurry and didn't show much apart from the varying heights of the three males. Even zooming in, he couldn't tell what the tattoos were supposed to be.

Looking at Jane, he said, "I appreciate your work on getting these, but until we can get a clearer view, these are a dead end for now."

Shrugging, Jane replied, "You never know. The photo may prove useful later, even without a clearer version. If you see three men of those heights, and tattoos in the same places, it's highly likely they're a match. There can't be that many men who match that description around here, unless there's a dragon hunter lookalike plot afoot."

"Don't be ridiculous. The bastards aren't going to take the time to find body doubles."

Jane winked. "That means you agree with me about the photo being useful." Jane's phone beeped, and she tapped it a few times before adding, "Wren found something at the farm with the first disappearance. Who knows, maybe that'll lead us to Delia. We need to hurry to the area where you can shift."

"Are you sure you're all right to fly that way again?"

Steel flickered in her gaze. "Having my heart in my stomach will be worth it if we end up finding your sister."

Not for the first time, Kai wondered how he deserved a mate like Jane.

His beast spoke up. *As I've said before, she's ours. Believe in her. Jane will grow old with us.*

As much as Kai had doubted bringing Jane along, their investigation seemed to be doing him good. The more determined Jane was to find his sister, the more faith he had that she would always stay with him. After all, a female wasn't going to go out of her way to face fears or put her life on the line for a male she planned to leave.

His dragon roared. *Stop with those thoughts. We are Jane's as much as she is ours. Hurry up and go to the area where we can shift so that we can keep working.*

He kissed Jane gently. "Do you think you can match my pace or should I carry you? I'm going to run."

She tilted her head. "I've been working out more, so I should be able to keep up. Let's find out."

As Jane turned and dashed toward the clearing, Kai ran after her. Nothing stirred a dragonman's blood like a chase. Once his sister was safe, he would have to try it with Jane in a remote location so he could catch her and show

44

his mate how much he loved her.

Not that he needed more motivation to find Delia. But any excuse to spend time with his mate was something he'd also fight for.

CHAPTER FIVE

While riding in a blasted basket was better than being carried via dragon talons, the instant one of Snowridge's Protectors released Jane's basket on solid ground, she jumped out and ran toward the edge of the landing area.

She thought she'd become more accustomed to flying, but it seemed she didn't mind only when Kai carried her.

However, she wasn't an idiot and about to throw a tantrum for not having her mate escort her back to Snowridge. Kai, Wren, and Eira had gone to further investigate the identical tire tracks they'd found at both of the farms. Snowridge's tracker, a female Protector named Carys, had taken Jane's place in the investigation. With Jane's regular human hearing and senses, she would have been a burden and only slowed them down.

Not that she was going to sit back and do nothing. Jane's gut said that someone had probably helped Delia with money or transportation to get off Snowridge. From what she'd heard, Delia would sometimes sneak away with friends but was caught more often than not. While there was a small chance Kai's sister had done the deed alone, Jane wouldn't dismiss any possibility.

So she was going to retrace her sister-in-law's steps. It would give her something to do and help her forget to worry about Kai.

Well, to mostly forget. As skilled as her mate was, if he ended up finding a dragon hunter hideout, there was always the chance he could be injured, or worse.

The hunter bastards didn't play fair and wouldn't think twice about using drugs or even an electrical blast gun to take down a dragon. If at all possible, they wouldn't kill him straight away since dragon's blood was valuable. But she'd heard from Nikki Gray about how the dragon hunters had drained one of Stonefire's Protectors to death. She clenched her fingers at the thought of her golden dragon-man being subjected to the same.

No. Everyone was better prepared than during that old incident, as well as being fully aware of the dragon hunters' barbarous tactics. Kai would take care of himself.

Taking a deep breath, she headed toward the main entrance inside the mountain and was greeted by Kai's mother, Lily. The older woman blurted, "What did you find out?"

She could sugar coat the facts, but she owed Lily the truth. "We know who Delia was searching for, but we're still not sure where she is."

Lily bobbed her head. "That's at least one step closer to finding my daughter."

Jane resisted blinking. "I had always wondered where Kai had got his levelheadedness from."

Lily wrapped an arm around her waist and guided them inside the rock. "I wasn't always this way. However, Kai's father was, and it rubbed off on me a little. He may not have been my true mate, but I loved him." She gave a sad smile. "I only wished Kai could remember more about him. He was a brave male, just like our son."

Kai rarely talked about his father, mostly because he'd been eight years old when his dad had died and didn't remember a lot. "Once all of this is sorted, you're going to have to tell me some more stories. Kai may be too stubborn to ask for them, but I know he yearns to hear more about his dad, too."

"That I can easily do." Lily gave her a gentle squeeze. "So, Kai mentioned on the phone something about you digging around for information here as well. Tell me what you need, and I'll help in any way that I can."

They turned the corner of the corridor and entered Lily's home. Once the door closed, Jane asked, "I'm trying to retrace Delia's steps. Her file only mentioned going to classes and not coming back from her lunch. I thought maybe her teachers might know or at least overheard something."

"I'll give you a list of her teachers."

Lily hesitated. Jane raised her eyebrow. "What don't you want to tell me?"

"How do you do that? Figure out that I'm hiding something?"

She shrugged. "It's a gift. But just tell me everything, Lily. Hiding even the smallest detail could make all the difference in the world."

Lily searched her gaze and finally sighed. "I was hoping to spare you the anger, but most of Delia's morning classes are taught by Maggie Jones."

She blinked before narrowing her eyes. "As in the same Maggie Jones who stomped on Kai's heart all those years ago?"

"While I appreciate your protective nature, you can't win against a dragon-shifter, Jane. Not even a soft-voiced one like Maggie. Remember that when you see her."

Jane took a deep breath and counted to three. Usually only her brother could stir her temper. "You're right, of course. It's just that dragonwoman's actions still affect

Kai." Jane debated sharing more, but as Lily merely waited patiently, she decided to blurt out, "No matter what I say or do, Kai thinks I'm going to leave him one day."

Lily gave a sad smile. "For all his alpha, Protector image, my son has always had a secret sensitive side. You've healed him better than I ever could have, Jane. I have faith that one day you'll chase away his doubts. Deep down, he probably knows that you're here to stay. But until that small part of him finally accepts that he didn't drive Maggie away, only her cowardliness did, he'll continue to be his own worst enemy."

Jane was used to being the strong woman who stood up to anything. But in that second, she didn't try to hide her insecurities. "I only hope that he'll heal fully one day. I'm not sure what else I can do."

Patting her arm, Lily added, "Don't worry. As soon as you two have a child, he should wise up."

Jane kept a smile pasted on her face but inwardly frowned. Having a baby to convince Kai that she would stay with him wasn't the best idea; a child should be wanted simply for them. There had to be another way.

Still, she couldn't bear to smash Lily's dreams of being a grandmother yet again, so she said, "Thanks for listening. I'll talk with Kai about this, but it's nice to share things with someone else who understands him well."

"Oh, I think you know him better than I do these days. He's lucky to have you, Jane Hartley."

Lily engulfed her in a hug and Jane wrapped her arms around her mother-in-law. "I think we need to come visit more often."

The older dragonwoman pulled back. "What would be even better is if you brought your parents here sometime. I've met Rafe—he's as bad as a dragonman when it comes to temper and alphaness, if I may say so—but not your parents. Snowridge's leader owes me a few favors, even after all of this, and I'd happily call them in for the Hartleys."

Bobbing her head, Jane answered, "Once we find Delia, I'll work on it."

"Good luck, child. If Maggie gives you any trouble, you call me immediately, do you hear?"

Despite Lily's soft appearance, there was no doubting the steel in her voice. "I will. Tell me where to find her and I'll start straight away."

As Lily gave her directions, Jane's heart rate ticked up. She'd put off this meeting long enough. It was high time for her to talk with the mysterious Maggie Jones. The trick would be focusing on Delia and not allowing the dragonwoman to provoke her, if she tried. Jane knew little about the dragonwoman, but all of that was about to change.

⌇⌇⌇

Kai wished he could soar over the area in his dragon form to find the truck they were looking for, but they couldn't risk being spotted and scaring away their possible targets.

So he followed Carys as she led them along the country road north of Dolgellau. Thanks to the abundance of trees to either side of the road, it was easy to mostly stay out of sight.

The brown-haired dragonwoman with green eyes stopped in her tracks and glanced to the left. She waved in the same direction. "They turned off the road here."

Kai scanned the area. The dirt road went through open spaces to a farmhouse in the distance. Not even his dragon eyesight could make out the details, so he took a pair of high-powered binoculars from his pack and zeroed in on the farmhouse.

In addition to the old two-story structure, there were a number of outbuildings and a large barn. While there was no truck in sight, several of the buildings were large enough to hide one inside.

Lowering his binoculars, he looked at the three other dragon-shifters. "Do you think any of the Snowridge farmers will know who these people are?"

Eira shook her head. "I doubt it. Few of the human farmers want anything to do with the dragon ones. Not to mention flying is restricted in this area to avoid spooking the animals."

Kai's dragon spoke up. *We need a human to look into it.*

Jane is English. Her accent will throw up a huge red flag.

There has to be a Welsh human who will help us.

Kai went through the few Welsh people he knew, both human and dragon, and finally remembered one. *Trahern's doctor friend, Emily Davies, is human.*

But she's from Cardiff. Welsh accents might all sound the same to me, but I'm sure the local people will notice.

Trying to find someone is too time-consuming. We'll have to do this a different way.

He focused back on the three dragon-shifters. "As much as I want to charge in and search the grounds, we should wait here in the tree cover. Once the truck exits and Carys can confirm the tracks, then we can try sneaking onto the grounds for evidence. Once we have it, we can call for backup."

"And if the truck never exits?" Wren asked.

Kai focused on Carys. "How sure are you of your tracking abilities?"

The dragonwoman placed her hands on her hips. "No other dragon has bested me yet in Wales." She narrowed her eyes at Wren. "And you know that."

Wren put up his hands. "I'm just trying to be prepared, Carys. You're skilled, but for all we know, they have tunnels. Wasn't that what you found near Carlisle previously, Kai, when you went after the dragon hunters there?"

Evie Marshall, the eventual mate of Stonefire's clan leader, had been kidnapped along with Nikki and another Protector named Charlie. Part of the rescue plan had involved using tunnels that the dragon hunters had dug for escape routes.

"Yes, but the formerly based Carlisle group have huge numbers and resources. It seems unlikely the same would happen here. I say we wait and if nothing shows up by nightfall, one or two of us can try looking around undetected."

Carys nodded. "I'll be one of them. I may spot something you can't see."

Kai jumped in before the others could talk. "And since Delia is my sister, I should be the other investigator, unless Wren or Eira have problems with that?"

"No, it's better for us to contact Snowridge for backup if needed anyway," Eira answered.

"Right, then let's settle in and each take different sections. Wren and Eira, go further south and keep an eye on the road. Carys and I will keep watch on the farm and surrounding open areas."

Kai was thankful that Eira and Wren went without complaint. It couldn't be easy for them to accept orders from another clan's Protector.

His dragon spoke up. *If they know the details concerning Evie's rescue, then they've certainly looked into our past work. They know we can deliver.*

Knowing someone is skilled and following their orders without hesitation are two different things.

Not to a dragon. Their dragon halves will keep them in line.

Kai snorted. *That's assuming everyone is as stubborn as you.*

Aren't all dragons stubborn?

Fair point. Now, be quiet. I need to pay attention.

As Kai watched the farmhouse and the outlying buildings, he also kept his ears open. If he so much as heard a child's scream, he would have enough grounds to look into it and avoid the DDA's ire in the aftermath.

Or, so he hoped.

No. He'd worry about DDA politics later. Even if it landed him in jail, he'd rescue his sister and the missing children. No one should endure the same fate as others that had been captured in the past, most especially children.

⁂

Jane stood at the entrance of the large cavern-like room and watched the quiet dragonwoman with dark hair.

From Maggie's soft-spoken voice to her slightly shorter than average stature for a dragon-shifter, Jane tried to imagine Kai with the woman. But every time she tried, she only saw Kai tiptoeing around her and keeping his alpha nature in check.

In other words, he was never allowed to be his true self.

How could fate have ever thought she was Kai's best chance for happiness, Jane had no bloody idea.

Still, no matter how much Jane disliked Maggie for hurting Kai, walking up to her and punching her in the face would be counterproductive. Besides, Maggie had never tried to entice Kai back. Hell, she'd barely even glanced at him whenever she and Kai had visited Snowridge in the past.

As Jane would tell Rafe if he'd wanted to do the same thing to one of Nikki's former lovers, she needed to grow the fuck up and focus on what was important—helping Delia.

A bell rang and the young dragon-shifter students picked up their bags and exited the room. According to Lily, Maggie would be free from now until after lunch.

Taking a deep breath, Jane moved from her hiding spot near the entrance and waltzed into the room.

Maggie looked up at the sound of her footsteps. Her pupils flashed to slits and back before she asked, "What do you need, Jane?"

"So you know who I am."

"Everybody on Snowridge does."

When Maggie didn't elaborate, Jane decided to steer the conversation toward her objective. "I'm here on an official matter, Ms. Jones. Delia went missing after your class and I need to know if she mentioned where she was going."

Maggie moved to her teacher's desk and sat behind it. "So you immediately thought I'd done something to drive Delia away."

Jane frowned. "I didn't say that. I'm just trying to get a better picture of what happened that day."

Maggie looked away, and it took everything Jane had not to growl and demand an answer. She couldn't afford to scare the dragonwoman and possibly miss out on information pertinent to her case.

The woman finally met her gaze again. "I may have mentioned a secret exit that the Protectors use to escape, but I didn't tell her to go looking for it."

"How did you know about this exit?"

She half expected for Maggie to bow her head and keep quiet. However, she answered, "My late mate's brother is a

Protector and he mentioned it to me once."

"Late mate?" Jane echoed.

"Yes. My mate died a few weeks ago, of a dragon-related disease."

As Jane's mind whirred, she noted the lack of grief in Maggie's eyes. She should keep her mouth shut, but her curiosity won out. "By your lack of mourning I'm guessing you didn't love him."

"No. Although he was good to me whilst alive." Maggie cleared her throat. "Is there anything else? Otherwise, I have lessons to prepare."

Maggie may be soft-spoken, but if she were weak in her youth, she'd mostly outgrown it.

Her first impulse was to tell Maggie to leave Kai alone. Jane had no idea if her kiss would still initiate the mate-claim frenzy or not. Dragon-shifters could move past a true mate, but Jane had no bloody idea how long it took.

But then she remembered Kai's loving glance, and it chased away her fears. Jane trusted Kai. Even if Maggie tried something, Kai would remain faithful.

A small niggle of doubt warned otherwise, but Jane pushed it away. Otherwise she might never find out what she needed. "If you mentioned the secret door, then I imagine Delia told you why she might need it. Can you share anything about that?"

Shrugging, Maggie rearranged a few stacks of paper. "She wanted to investigate something, to try to imitate you." Maggie's dark gaze met her own. "If anything, this is your fault. It's hard for a human to understand, but drag-on-shifter teenagers are always out to prove themselves. Delia is trying to prove herself to you."

Jane clenched her fingers. "Says the woman who told her how to escape. Hate me if you like, but risking a child's life to get at me is unforgivable."

"Kai will find her, but he'll blame you for it all. Maybe then he'll finally understand why humans and dragons should never mate."

She closed the distance between them. "Kai will easily see how a woman who broke his heart wanted to hurt his current love. What happened with Kai is your fault, Maggie. If you think there's a second chance with Kai, then you don't understand him at all."

"I'm not about to discuss dragon matters with a human. I've told you all that I know. You'd better leave before I mention to my clan leader how a human is trying to scare me into saying what she wants to hear."

The urge to punch Maggie returned, but Lily's warning about not being able to win against a dragon-shifter came back to her.

Jane may not be able to win a physical fight, but she could win the long game. Once Kai returned, they should be able to find a way to use Maggie's pettiness to ensure she got what she deserved. Putting any young at risk was a crime with dragon-shifters. Or, so it was on Stonefire. She imagined it was the same on Snowridge.

Maggie Jones would get her comeuppance in the end.

Jane took a step back. "This isn't over."

Shrugging, Maggie raised her brows. "It's your word against mine. I don't know how things are done on Stonefire, but Snowridge puts clan above strangers."

Jane wanted to take out her phone and show she'd recorded the interview, as she always did, to review later. However, Jane would allow Maggie to think she was safe.

Turning around, she strode out the classroom and down the corridor. It seemed Jane and even Kai had underestimated Maggie's abilities. She'd ensure that neither one of them ever did so again.

CHAPTER SIX

*K*ai and Carys had kept to the trees and watched the area until nightfall. When the sun finally set and nothing had happened, they made their way toward the farmhouse and other buildings. Eira and Wren were posted at two different spots to keep watch and alert them to anyone coming their way.

Thanks to his dragon-shifter eyesight, Kai could see every rock or even cigarette butt on the ground despite the near-darkness. The key was to make as little sound as possible and to avoid any potential booby traps. Kai didn't think they'd have sophisticated security systems, but he kept an eye out for them as well.

Light shone through one of the windows in the farmhouse on the ground level. However, as they approached, he didn't hear any talking, footsteps, or other signs of human habitation. He signaled for Carys to investigate the perimeter of the house while he went to the barn.

As his dragon always did on important missions, he remained silent inside Kai's head but lent his observation skills and would let him know if he spotted or heard anything.

Closing the distance to the stone building of the barn, Kai sniffed the air. Instead of animal dung, hay, or dirt, he smelled something chemical he couldn't name.

Since he'd dealt with his fair share of explosives in his army days and could identify them by scent, he ruled them out, too. However, ever since his clan had been targeted with drugs that made dragon halves take over and go wild, Kai had learned to be cautious of any chemical he couldn't name. When he had the chance, he needed to talk with Dr. Sid and the other doctors on Stonefire so that he could obtain a sample of the drug and have his Protectors memorize the smell.

Scanning the side of the barn, he counted a few long, narrow slits on the sides in addition to the set of wide, wooden doors. One of the ventilation slits was on ground level, so Kai crouched down and crept to just below it. The silence made him suspicious.

Careful not to disturb the earth and make noise, Kai rose slowly until he could peek through the opening. A large, white truck sat at the far side of the room. Sweeping the room with his eyes, he noticed a thin line of light shining from behind a closed door.

His dragon spoke up. *We need to look inside.*

I know. Give me a bloody moment.

Dropping down, Kai quietly moved to the wide door. The hinges weren't well-oiled, which meant they'd make too much sound. He continued moving until he turned the corner and examined the other side of the barn. One of the windows didn't have any glass in it. While high up, it was his best option for getting inside.

When he reached just below it, he jumped up and just managed to grab the ledge. He slowly pulled himself up. As he attempted to lean inside the window to check the surroundings one more time, something scratched his arm. He dismissed it as remnants of the former window. However, when he finished his sweep of the interior, his grip slipped. He tried to catch himself, but his fingers barely responded. Kai fell and managed to tumble into a somersault to avoid making too much noise.

Inside his mind, his dragon curled into a ball. *So much noise. Make it stop.*

Kai heard nothing.

Carys appeared at his side. One look at him and she crouched down, slung his arm around her shoulders, and helped him up.

As his dragon started to roar, Kai barely paid attention to what was happening. Only when he heard Carys's voice was he able to note they were back inside the cover of the trees.

"What's wrong?" she asked.

"Scratch on my arm..." His dragon roared louder. "Something is wrong. Get me back."

His beast flicked his wings and pushed to the front of Kai's mind. He managed to whisper, "Drug me," before he was tossed inside a mental prison and forced to watch his dragon thrash about uncontrollably.

Carys placed a hand over his mouth and quickly extracted a pre-filled syringe from one of her pockets. Kai's dragon bit her palm, but she merely grunted and stuck the needle into his skin.

In the next instant, Carys flew several feet into a tree. To her credit, she didn't cry out but rolled right back at him.

Kai wanted to stop his beast, but could do nothing but pound against the invisible prison.

Carys reached him with another needle in her hand. Kai had no idea if the first one hadn't worked or wasn't doing anything.

Kai's dragon lunged at her, but Carys sidestepped and swept his leg. He faltered and she jumped on his back with an arm around his neck. His dragon growled, but Kai could feel the prick of another syringe. His dragon continued to buck their human form until Carys was thrown against another tree trunk.

His dragon turned their body toward her, but as he took a step, he faltered and fell to his knees. After another second, the world went black as Kai silently hoped his dragon hadn't just alerted the inhabitants to their presence.

～◦⌒◦◦⌒◦～

Jane stood with Lily and Gareth Owens on the outskirts of the landing area. Snowridge's leader had told them Kai had been injured, but nothing more.

While her mate had been hurt in the line of duty countless times before, Rhydian not telling her or Lily the details didn't bode well.

Lily put an arm around Jane's shoulders. "I'm sure it's nothing, Jane. If he were dying, Rhydian would've said."

What Jane didn't mention was that there were worse fates than death for dragon-shifters. Between going rogue or inner dragons going silent, there were many things that could be wrong with Kai.

Not usually one to wring hands, she couldn't help but twist her fingers around each other. On Stonefire, she would already know what was going on. Being the outsider on Snowridge seemed to cause one complication after another.

A red dragon came into view. Behind it was a black dragon. Since Kai was a golden one, he had to be in his human form with one of the two beasts.

As they drew closer, Jane focused on the red dragon, which was slightly smaller and meant it was a female. From the way her hind legs were close to her body instead of down and behind, it meant the dragon was carrying something.

Soon enough she could make out a human form clutched in talons.

It was Kai.

Never taking her eyes off her mate, Jane watched as the red dragon made it to the landing area, hovered, and gently laid him on the ground. The instant the dragon moved away, Jane raced to her mate's side.

Kneeling down, she checked him for injuries. But beyond a scratch on his arm, she didn't notice anything else.

The red dragon had shifted back into Carys's human form. Jane looked at the dragonwoman. "What happened?"

The dragonwoman shrugged. "I'm not entirely sure. All I know is that his dragon took over and immediately treated me as an enemy. Kai mentioned the scratch, but nothing else."

Jane looked back to her mate and placed a hand on his chest to ground her. She'd never be able to help her dragonman if she broke down and lost focus.

Taking a deep breath, she leaned down and studied the scratch. The blood had already clotted and there was no apparent redness or puffiness. "Were there drones or special guns fired at you?"

"No. I saw Kai try to crawl through a barn window, and next thing I know, he fell to the ground. While I didn't have time to investigate the barn, there was a strange chemical smell wafting from it. Maybe long exposure to it knocked him out."

"Possibly." Jane moved her hand up his chest, his neck, and finally cupped his strong jaw. "I'd highly suggest a blood test and reaching out to Dr. Cassidy Jackson on Stonefire. I can't be sure, but this might be something we've dealt with before."

Before Carys could answer, Rhydian Griffith's voice filled the area. "I think we need to talk, Ms. Hartley."

Jane glanced up. "If you think I'm going to leave Kai's side, then I'm sorry, I'm going to have to say no, even if it means defying your orders."

"I wouldn't expect anything else of Kai's mate. But whilst the doctors examine him, you're going to tell me everything you think you know about this situation. Hovering at his side will only get in their way and delay their treatment. A clever female like yourself knows better."

The steel in Rhydian's voice made Jane want to bob her head, but as she stroked the late-day stubble on Kai's cheek, she found the strength to say, "I'll share as much as I can without asking my clan leader's permission."

Rhydian smiled. "Good girl. You might be human, but you seem to mostly understand our ways."

She nearly growled out she wasn't a girl, but instead, bit the inside of her cheek to keep silent. Certain battles weren't worth it.

A male wearing a white lab coat, denoting him as a clan doctor, rushed to the scene. Two other males carrying a stretcher trailed behind him. The doctor said, "I understand your concern for your mate, but we need to get him to my surgery as quickly as possible. Please stand aside."

Jane reluctantly backed away and watched as the three men maneuvered Kai onto a stretcher. Even though all dragon-shifters were naturally stronger than humans, the two males with the stretcher between them had to grunt with effort to carry her muscled mate away.

Rhydian motioned for her to precede him. She should say something diplomatic, but all she cared about was Kai's well-being, and she half ran to keep up with the dragon medical staff.

They carried him to a different entrance off the landing

area that Jane hadn't noticed before. Inside was a large cavern stocked with medical equipment. One large dragon slept at the far side.

She'd barely noted the rare white hide of the sleeping beast before she followed the staff into a room.

The doctor motioned for Jane to keep her distance. "Let me do my job."

Jane crossed her arms and watched as the doctor started his examination. Rhydian's voice filled her ear. "From everything I know about Kai, he'll be fine. He may not be of my clan, but Lily is an important part of Snowridge and I'll do anything to help her. She's given my cousin happiness I never thought he'd have."

She glanced at Snowridge's leader. Sincerity shone in his eyes. "Are you talking about Lily's mate, Gareth? He's your cousin?"

"Yes. Now, tell me as much as you're able about all of this and your guesses as to what caused his condition."

Jane looked at Kai and watched the medical staff work as she answered, "All of the British and Irish dragon clans know of the drone attacks on Stonefire, which means you should, too."

"Yes, the ones that shot drugs into dragons, making them go wild."

"For the most part," Jane replied. "The dragon halves took over and reverted to their animalistic instincts. Trahern reached out to a doctor here for a possible cure. Some sort of moss that's found in Wales."

Dr. Trahern Lewis was a Snowridge doctor who had moved to Stonefire earlier in the year.

When Rhydian grunted for her to continue, she did. "Carys mentioned a strong chemical smell coming from the barn they were investigating. Kai has a scratch on his arm, and while it's just a guess at this point, it could be that the same or a similar chemical got into his blood-stream via the scratch." She darted a look at Rhydian. "I'm not sure if you can answer my question, but have your Protectors found anything related to the drone attacks or dragons going wild around here?"

"We've never been attacked this way before, that much I can tell you," Rhydian stated.

"I'm not going to try to order you to do anything, sir, as I respect your role as clan leader, but I think more Protectors should be sent to investigate the area."

Rhydian smiled. "You're unlike any human female I've met before. Aren't you afraid of overstepping your bounds and causing strife between our clans?"

"If you're smiling, then no, I think I'm okay."

The dragonman snorted. "You're definitely an odd human." She growled and he put up a hand. "More Protectors are already on the way. If something can take down your mate this easily, my guess is that there is more to the farm than the smell of chemicals. Someone means to harm my clan, and I won't allow it."

"And what about reaching out to Dr. Sid on Stonefire?"

Sighing, Rhydian replied, "Let's hear what our doctor has to say first. After all, he knows about the moss and ensuing compound that was used on Stonefire. Trahern may be with Stonefire now, but he still shares medical knowledge with our clan. Something to do with your Dr. Sid's ambitious, worldwide plan." He moved his gaze to the doctor's back. "Maelon, what did you find?"

The male doctor turned around. "Beyond the scratch on his arm and a slightly erratic heart beat, everything else is normal. I'll test his blood and check it against Trahern's data. In the meantime, I'm going to allow the sedative to wear off so I can see his reaction. If Kai wakes up violent, I'll sedate him again. If you could post two Protectors in his room, in case he breaks his restraints, I would appreciate it."

Jane spoke up before Rhydian. "You're going to restrain him?"

Maelon shifted his gaze to her. "From what I've heard, Stonefire did the same to those hit with the darts from the drones."

"Sorry, you're right." Jane stared at Kai's still body. "But I want to stay with him."

Rhydian jumped in. "There's nothing you can do here, Ms. Hartley. Go back to Lily's place and rest. We may need your help further regarding Delia's search."

"I can help just as easily from here."

Maelon chuckled. "Rhydian, trust me, mates rarely take the suggestion to rest when they should in these types of situations."

Jane managed to tear her gaze from Kai. "Even I know that, Doctor...?"

Maelon put out a hand. "I'm Dr. Maelon Perry, Snowridge's head doctor."

Shaking his hand, Jane blurted out, "You seem young to be head doctor."

The black-haired, brown-eyed doctor smiled. "If you listen to my orders, then maybe I'll tell you the why behind it."

Even though Jane had just met Maelon, his presence brought calmness. Most doctors seemed to have that characteristic. She finally released her grip. "Consider it a deal, Doctor Perry."

"Good. Then allow the nurses to finish restraining Kai and then you can sit at his side. However, I will also put a temporary bed in here for you. Promise me now that you'll use it if you get tired."

At the steel in the doctor's voice, she said, "I will."

"Right, then let's get everything finalized. Once I have the blood results, I'll let you both know what I find."

Jane turned toward Rhydian. "I also want to know what you find at that farm." Rhydian raised an eyebrow and Jane added, "Please."

"You may amuse me, Ms. Hartley, but that will only go so far before I start reprimanding you. After all, you are a guest on my clan. Understood?"

Since she couldn't risk angering the clan leader, she murmured, "Yes."

"Then stay here and I'll let you know what I can via your mobile phone. Now excuse me, I have matters to attend. Your clan leader is waiting on details from me."

Once Snowridge's leader exited the room, Dr. Perry gave a few last minute instructions to his nurses before doing the same. It took everything Jane had to stay back and watch the nurses draw blood and restrain Kai.

The second they finished, she was at his bedside and gently brushing his forehead. "Whatever happens, I'll be here, Kai. Maybe when you're well again, you'll finally realize that there isn't anything I wouldn't do to stay by your side. I love you."

Leaning down, she kissed his lips and settled into the chair next to the bed to do what she hated most—wait and see what happened.

CHAPTER SEVEN

*J*ane stood on the back of a flying dragon as it sailed through the rainbow-colored clouds. Despite her arms thrown wide, the wind wasn't more than a soft whisper against her skin.

For the first time, she started to understand why Kai loved flying so much.

However, before she could enjoy the sensation any longer, a roar cut through her dream and her eyes popped open.

Kai thrashed in his restraints on the bed. If that wasn't bad enough, a face she didn't want to see stood over him.

Maggie Jones gazed down at Kai with longing.

Jane jumped to her feet, but a pair of muscled arms wrapped around her from behind. She tried to throw her head back to make contact with her assailant's nose, but he easily dodged it. She spat out, "Let me go."

Maggie smiled at Jane. "For the next ten minutes, you're powerless, Jane Hartley. I hope you enjoy the show."

She vaguely remembered Maggie having a Protector cousin. The bastard must've sent the second guard away on an errand.

Maggie turned her attention back to Kai, who was struggling even more against his restraints.

His pupils were slitted, meaning his dragon was in charge. And given his jerky, erratic movements, his beast wasn't in his right mind.

As Maggie lowered her head toward Kai's lips, Jane stopped breathing. "No."

The dragonwoman ignored her to murmur to Kai, "I should've done this a long time ago. I'm finally ready to bring you the happiness you deserve, with someone who understands all of you."

Maggie closed the distance to Kai's lips, and Jane tried again to smack her restrainer's head. When that failed, she used her heel to stomp his foot.

But the dragonman merely grunted and tightened his hold on her.

The bitch was trying to steal her mate and Jane was powerless to do anything.

When Maggie raised her head, Jane held her breath and hoped with everything she had that Kai's dragon had been truthful when saying Jane was all that they needed.

Because if Maggie Jones started a mate-claim frenzy and stole Kai away from her, Jane would die a little inside. Mate-claim frenzies always resulted in pregnancy, which meant Kai would have a child. His duty would want to see it through with Maggie.

For the first time, she wondered if she'd been a fool for trying to win a dragonman's heart when fate had decreed that another was his best chance at happiness.

But she quickly pushed the doubt aside. Kai was her dragonman. She had to believe that his love for her was stronger than a dragon's instinct.

⁓⁓⁓

Kai regained consciousness inside the mental prison.

His head was foggy and he could barely make out his dragon's form at the front of their mind.

Female voices drifted through the space, but he couldn't make out what they were saying at first. Then a voice he hadn't heard in over a decade rang out clear. "I should've done this a long time ago. I'm finally ready to bring you the happiness you deserve, with someone who understands all of you."

Confusion set in. Why would Maggie say that to him?

His awareness fully returned as strange lips touched his.

Roaring, his beast thrashed wildly. The drugs must've affected his dragon severely since he didn't speak, but only roared and bellowed, trying to get free of the restraints around their arms, middle, and legs.

Not sure if his dragon would hear him, Kai shouted, *She isn't for us. Remember Jane.*

As if on cue, Jane's voice reached his ears. "Kai! If you can hear me, help!"

The desire to claim a female hit him at full blast. He fucking hoped it wasn't for Maggie. *We love Jane.*

Still ignoring him, his dragon yelled as he finally broke the restraints around their upper body. A split second later, he extended a talon and ripped through the ones around their waist and legs. Jumping to a crouch on the bed, his dragon hissed and looked at Maggie.

Shit. Kai pounded against his invisible prison. He couldn't allow fate to ruin his life and take away the other half of his heart.

Then his beast shifted their gaze to Jane, who was being held captive from behind by a male dragon-shifter.

His dragon finally spoke inside their head, *He dies.*

As he lunged at the male, Kai punched his mental prison wall once, twice, and on the third time, it cracked. He couldn't allow his beast to kill anyone or he'd never hold Jane in his arms again.

With his dragon still in control, their human form punched the male dragon-shifter in the nose and pulled Jane away, until she stood behind them. His beast clocked the male again, and he dropped to the floor. With a growl, he moved to pin the male down.

Despite the effects of the drug and his beast's raging nature, Kai drew on every speck of discipline he possessed to slowly create a mental cage for his dragon. It was hard to ignore the sound of his fist against the other male's jaw, but he somehow managed it.

His future with Jane depended on it.

He finally lunged at his beast inside his head and wrestled with him. In their physical forms, the dragon would easily win. However, inside their brain, they were the same size.

They rolled, and Kai managed to steer them toward the cage. When Jane cried out, "What the fuck?" he tossed his dragon inside and quickly sealed up the opening.

Fully in control of his human body again, Kai turned to see Maggie holding a talon to Jane's neck.

He didn't have time to wonder where the shy girl of his younger years had gone. "Maggie, what are you doing?"

"Humans are weak. She'll break, Kai. I'm going to save you the heartache later and just end it now."

With Maggie's pupils flashing from slits to round and back again, Kai remained where he stood. Kai may be able to control his beast because of his military discipline, but Maggie lacked it.

And as she pressed a little harder against Jane's neck, a tiny drop of blood cascaded down her skin.

His dragon threw himself against his cage, and again. If Kai didn't entice Maggie away from Jane, his dragon would break free and Maggie would kill his mate before he could do anything.

As much as the idea of wanting Maggie made him recoil, he needed to trick her. He may not be as good an actor as Jane, but if Maggie had convinced herself killing Jane would bring him into her arms, she'd probably believe anything she wanted to hear.

Kai put out a hand. "Killing anyone, even a human, means we'll be separated, Maggie, love. Let her go and take my hand. Then we can go wherever you like and be together."

It took everything Kai had to keep his gaze on Maggie and not share a glance with Jane. He only hoped his clever mate would understand what he was doing.

"Then kiss me to prove it, Kai. If I believe you truly want me, then I'll release the human and flee with you. Trick me, and she dies."

He nodded. To protect Jane's life, Kai would pretend he wanted Maggie.

Ignoring his dragon's bellow at kissing anyone but their mate, Kai slowly closed the distance between them. From the corner of his eyes, he saw Jane's face. She had a frown and tightly pressed lips, but it was an act—she lacked the usual fire in her eyes that denoted her anger.

Still, as he approached Maggie, the thought of kissing the woman who broke his heart all those years ago made him want to bolt in the opposite direction so he could run to her leader and report her. He wouldn't ruin his or Jane's life by hitting her. No, she deserved to go to prison and know she put herself there.

But he needed Jane safe and sound first.

He stopped a few inches in front of Maggie and tried his best to smile. He lightly caressed her cheek. "Hello, Maggie."

71

"Kiss me, Kai. With my mate gone, nothing stands in the way."

Except for Jane, but he kept that thought to himself.

He moved in closer. "Nothing at all."

"Prove it. Show me how much you want me."

He mentally asked for Jane's forgiveness as he closed the distance and touched his lips to Maggie's.

The feel of her skin against him did nothing but make him want to step away and wipe away her taste. She tasted like rotten fish compared to the sweet honey of his beautiful Jane.

Still, he needed to convince Maggie, so he probed her lips with his tongue and entered her mouth. When she lightly caressed his tongue with hers, he wanted to gag.

Think of Jane. Getting her away from Maggie was all that mattered and was worth any price.

Despite it going against every honorable instinct he had to be faithful to his mate, Kai wrapped an arm around Maggie's waist. He continued kissing her for a few more seconds before pulling away. He did his best to keep his tone husky as he asked, "How was that?"

"A good start. But I need to be sure."

Before he could do more than blink, Maggie moved her talon to Jane's shoulder and stabbed her.

He barely noted Jane's scream as he grabbed Maggie's wrist and slowly pulled out the talon. The second it was free, Jane slumped to the floor. Kai quickly flipped Maggie onto her stomach and kept her hands restrained behind her back.

Part of him wanted to yell at Maggie, but he looked to Jane holding her hand over her shoulder.

There was a lot of blood.

Kai roared, "Nurse, help!"

But no one came. Odd, since dragon-shifter nurses always kept an ear out for trouble inside the surgery.

Kai reached up to one of the restraints on the bed next to him and tore it off. Quickly tying Maggie's hands to give him a few minutes before she tried shifting, he moved to Jane's side. "This is going to hurt, love, but I need to get you out of here and find a doctor."

She sucked in a breath. "Then do it."

Gently as he could, Kai scooped Jane up and held her against his chest. Not wasting another moment, he moved to the door, kicked it out, and took Jane into the corridor.

As he ran toward the reception area, he expected to run into one of the nurses or Dr. Perry. However, he saw no one, not even when he reached the reception area.

Something was wrong.

He chanced a glance at Jane. Her pale skin made his stomach twist. If he didn't find somewhere safe where he could use his field medic training to staunch the bleeding, she could die.

Racing out of the surgery's front entrance, he barreled down the hall, searching for an open door.

⌒◦⌒◦⌒◦

The throbbing pain in Jane's shoulder almost made her forget about Kai kissing Maggie.

Almost.

She knew he'd done it to save her. Maggie may not understand Kai's body language, but he'd clenched one of his fists as he kissed Maggie. Compared to when he kissed Jane, his actions had been wooden.

Jane wasn't prone to pettiness or hysterics, but if Maggie ever appeared in front of her again, she would chance it and take the bitch down.

Kai turned a corner, and the motion jolted her shoulder. Jane hissed as pain shot through her body.

"Hang on just a bit longer, love. I just need to put distance between us and the surgery, to make sure we're safe," Kai murmured.

She was about to say she understood when he stopped suddenly. She bit her lip and turned her face toward Kai's chest to keep from screaming.

It was only when Kai placed her on something soft a minute later that Jane realize she'd closed her eyes. She tried to open them, but they were unusually heavy.

Kai said, "One second and I'll help you, love. I just need to reinforce the door and fetch a few supplies."

For the brief moment his heat disappeared from her side, Jane shivered. Just as she finally managed to open her eyes, Kai was next to her again. "I need to check your shoulder and see if I can stop the bleeding. I won't lie, it's going to hurt. Are you ready?"

She bobbed her head and steeled herself for what was to come.

Kai ripped the remnants of her shirt to expose the wound. Jane glanced down and her previous meal threatened to come up.

While she could handle seeing a little blood, she had a gaping wound with more exposed tissue than she wanted to see. No wonder she was on the verge of passing out. "Am I going to die?"

"No fucking way I'm going to let that happen." He took some towels with him as he raced inside a small room adjacent to what she surmised was a toilet and came back with wet towels.

He dabbed around her wound and spots started to fill her vision. "Kai, I'm going to pass out."

"Stay with me as long as possible, Janey."

"I—" Lightheadedness made the room sway. "I love you,

Kai. I hope you know that."

"Don't you dare say goodbye to me, Jane Hartley."

Someone pounded on the door.

Kai pressed a dry towel against her wound and she cried out. He murmured apologies as he quickly tied another piece of material around it.

The pounding intensified. Kai lightly traced her cheek before murmuring, "Stay with me a little longer, Janey."

She wanted to say she would, but it was becoming harder to keep her eyes open.

With a curse, Kai shouted, "Who is it?"

"Rhydian Griffiths. Open this bloody door, Kai Sutherland. That's an order."

As Kai moved to the door, Jane tried to reach a hand out to ask him to stay. However, she could do little more than watch Kai's back before the world went dark.

⁓⊶⌇⊶⌇⊶⁓

Leaving Jane to open the door was the hardest thing Kai had done in years. But if there was anyone who could help him and his mate, it was Snowridge's clan leader.

Kai moved his temporary barricade and threw open the door. The instant it was open, he raced back to Jane's side.

She was unconscious.

Fuck. He glanced over his shoulder, but he didn't see any of the doctors or nurses he knew. "Jane needs medical attention straight away. I slowed down the bleeding, but she might need surgery."

"All of the on-duty medical staff are unconscious. I need to know what happened in there, Kai."

He cupped Jane's cheek and slowly moved his fingers to her carotid artery. Her heart beat was steady but slower than he liked. He finally answered, "I know you have at least one retired doctor here. Fetch him and I'll talk."

Rhydian signaled to one of his Protectors, who took out a mobile and went into the hallway. "Dr. Hughes will be along shortly. Now, start talking."

Kai never took his gaze from Jane as he answered, "I woke up to Maggie Jones kissing me and all hell broke loose." Kai rehashed the events before asking, "How did this happen, Rhydian? I trusted you, and now my mate could die."

"Not everyone welcomes humans as you do, Kai. I've learned to tolerate them out of necessity, but there are no human sacrifices here, nor have there been for quite a while. I suspect the children being kidnapped and everyone blaming the human dragon hunters was the final straw for the extremist few." He paused and his voice was quiet when he said, "In truth, I've had a hard enough time filling the ranks with new Protectors after what happened with Gwendolen Price."

During her time with the British Army, Gwendolen Price had fallen in love with a human soldier, become pregnant, and when injured during a mission, her human lover had sacrificed himself to save her. Shortly after, she had been discharged and had spent her time on Snowridge, raising her half-human daughter.

Rhydian added, "Lowering standards ultimately resulted in corruption, such as with Maggie's cousin. With my most trusted Protectors out looking for your sister and the missing children, the less reliable were left here. I accept full responsibility for the chaos."

Kai watched the rise and fall of Jane's chest. There was a lot he wanted to ask, but his mate's health was the most important thing to him at the moment. "Once Jane is out of danger, we're going to have a much longer conversation, Rhydian. Until then, I suggest you clean up the ranks of your Protectors."

"It's already being done. Rest assured that Maggie Jones will face trial for her transgressions."

At the mention of Maggie, his dragon roared and began thrashing once more. Kai couldn't risk his beast taking control, so he slowly reinforced the mental cage. By the time he finished, Dr. Arwel Hughes—the retired doctor who had helped Stonefire with finding a cure for the dragon madness drug—burst into the room with a bag in hand.

Despite his gray hair and slightly stooped shoulders, he pushed Kai aside and began removing the makeshift bandage.

"If there's anything I can do, Doctor, please tell me," Kai said.

Dr. Hughes didn't deviate from his task. "Just stay out of my way. If I need something from my bag, I'll ask and you can give it to me."

Kai gave the doctor room to do his work. He didn't know if Dr. Hughes had any experience with humans since his training days decades ago. But he was still better than no doctor at all.

Rather than worry about something he couldn't change, Kai focused on Jane's face. Even though she was unconscious, he would use every bit of stubbornness he possessed to will her to live.

Because a life without Jane would be worse than hell. He'd gone through it once when Maggie had rejected him and he'd survived. But Kai wasn't sure he could survive it again without Jane at his side.

CHAPTER EIGHT

Five hours later, Kai sat next to Jane's bed in the surgery, his mother at his side.

Jane was hooked up to various machines to monitor her vital signs as well as being connected to a drip for pain medication. The doctor was confident that she'd pull through, although a lot of physical therapy was in Jane's near future to help her recover full or nearly full use of her shoulder.

If Maggie had struck a few inches further down, she could've pierced a lung and Jane might've died.

His heart tightened at that thought. Despite her tough attitude, his human was fragile.

Since Kai had been given a dose of the special moss formula to erase the effects of the drug in his system, his dragon was out inside his mind and spoke up. *But she didn't die. Jane is alive, Maggie is in custody, and Rhydian is trying his best to clean house.*

Don't try to make me feel better, dragon. I fucked up by trusting Snowridge far sooner than I should have.

Rubbish. We've been here many times and met many of Snowridge's Protectors. We had no way of knowing that they always showed their best recruits to us and kept the unworthy hidden. Besides, Maggie fooled most of her clan with her skittish act. If they couldn't tell what she was up to, then there was no way we could've noticed it.

His dragon was right, but Kai wasn't going to stroke his ego just yet.

Kai had spent the last few hours focusing on Jane and reaching out to Bram, but now that he had a moment, he asked his dragon, *Why didn't you go into the mate-claim frenzy when Maggie kissed us?*

His beast huffed. *I don't want her. You should know that, but you never listen to me when it concerns this topic. True mate pulls fade with time. Jane is our human and will always be our mate.*

Raising Jane's hand to his lips, he kissed her warm fingers. "We'll get through this, Janey, I promise."

His mother spoke up. "Of course you will. You chose Jane without any instinct involved and fought to keep her. I only hope that you'll now stop doubting her and worrying that she'll leave."

He glanced at his mother. "How do you know I doubted anything?"

"You've always had a secret side, to doubt everything. You keep it hidden from the world, but I'm your mother. More than that, Jane told me. If all of this doesn't prove she's going to stay, then I don't know what will. Cherish her, Kai, and happiness will follow."

His dragon said, *I agree. Cherish her, but don't smother her.*

Says the overprotective dragon.

His beast merely huffed.

Kai was about to reply to his mother when her mobile phone chirped. She quickly answered it. "Hello?"

Because of Kai's hearing, he easily listened to the reply on the line. "Lily, this is Wren. We found Delia and she's alive."

"Alive?" Lily echoed.

"Yes, and before your fret, she'll live. But it's going to take some time to flush out all the drugs in her system."

Kai growled, leaned toward his mother's phone, and barked, "Instead of dangling bits of information, just tell us what's going on."

Lily clicked a button and the phone went to speaker. Wren's voice filled the room. "I can't say much over an unsecured line, but we'll be back on Snowridge within the hour. Eira will fetch you and bring you to us. We can divulge all the details then."

Since his mother sat still, Kai jumped in. "What about the missing children?"

"We have them, too. Again, I can't say anything else until I'm back on clan lands."

Lily cleared her throat. "Hurry, Wren. I need to see my baby girl."

"Of course, Lily. We'll return as quickly as possible."

The line went dead. Kai laid a hand on his mother's shoulder. "She's alive, Mum. That's all that matters."

She nodded. "I know, but there's more to the story and I'm afraid of what it is."

He pulled his mother to his side and hugged her. "We'll survive it together, Mum. Add in Jane and Gareth, who will also stand with us, and we'll be able to tackle anything."

His mum gave a choked laugh. "At least you've stopped pitying yourself. Jane would like that."

He stared at his mate's sleeping face. "Yes, she would. Although I think she'll be pissed to wake up and miss all the commotion with Delia's return."

"As much as I hate to say it, Kai, it's probably for the best that she's restricted to this room for now. Rhydian is still trying to weed out the human-hating extremists within the clan."

"Bastards."

"I agree, but cursing won't change anything."

His dragon spoke up. *I bloody well disagree. It's much easier to release anger with swearing.*

He ignored his beast to say, "Zain and Sebastian should be here from Stonefire at any minute. They'll protect Jane with their lives. More than that, I'd trust both of them with the other half of my heart."

Lily smiled. "I didn't know you were romantic."

"If there's one thing I've learned today, it's that Jane is my life. It's not romantic, but a fact that if she died, I'd go crazy and possibly rogue."

"Then we'll just have to take good care of your Janey."

Both man and beast agreed with that statement. As Kai and his mother fell into a comfortable silence, Kai memorized every line, freckle, and pore of Jane's face. Doing so helped him to focus and calm his mind.

Because he had a feeling that more shit was going to hit the fan soon enough once Delia and the others arrived back on Snowridge.

⟶∽⟵⟶∽⟵

Not for the first time, Rhydian Griffiths regretted succumbing to pressure from clan members to eschew anything human, if possible.

True, he had his own reasons for doing it. Namely, defending his human lover in his youth had earned him the scars on his face. Because of his past, he'd had to work extra hard to prove he had his clan's best interests at heart rather than his own. Winning the leadership trial had never been enough.

His dragon growled. *I still don't understand the need to hide our feelings. Lili should've been ours. Instead, they locked us up and chased her out of Wales.*

Liliwen Rosser had enticed Rhydian with her dark eyes and dark hair. Coupled with her laughter and zest for life, he had contemplated leaving the clan to claim her.

However, his mother and father had worked with his extended family to contain him, threaten the female, and drive them apart. Only his cousin Gareth had stood at his side.

Rhydian had only been twenty at the time, fresh out of the British Army. He'd challenged his uncles and lost badly.

The scars on his face reminded him every day of how changing the clan's prejudices didn't happen overnight.

His dragon chimed in. *But it might be time, especially if we form an alliance with Stonefire. Many of their humans have helped us, even here in Wales.*

We'll see, dragon. For the moment, we need to focus on Delia, the children, and cleaning up the clan. Otherwise, Bram will never send someone to foster, let alone risk his clan to help us.

Then hurry up and do the job. I'm tired of being isolated and spending most of our time inside the mountains. A dragon should be free and soaring in the skies.

Rhydian resisted pointing out that Snowridge had existed for the last several hundred years inside the mountains.

He reached the landing area and spotted Eira, Wren, and several other Protectors in the sky. As they made their final approach, he noticed a few makeshift baskets clutched in Wren and Eira's back talons.

It had to be Delia and the children.

Although as another trusted Protector, Delwyn, approached from the middle of the formation, Rhydian spotted another makeshift basket. Maybe there had been more children than just the few taken from his clan members.

Each dragon carefully laid down their package, be it baskets or crates of what he assumed to be chemicals confiscated from the farm near Dolgellau.

Since Maelon and his nurses had awoken and had been cleared for duty, they rushed toward the baskets. Rhydian followed closely on their heels.

The first one he approached contained Delia Owens. She was bound and wriggling, her pupils slitted.

It was hard to see his sweet, energetic second cousin so out of character.

Still, he allowed Maelon and his team to do their work and walked to the other two baskets. Inside one, he saw the missing children from the farms, unconscious. Rhydian motioned to one of the nurses. "Here, Olwenna. They need attention, too."

Without missing a beat, the female nurse came and started checking vital signs.

As much as he wanted to stay and watch, Rhydian needed to take in the entire situation, so he approached the third basket. Inside was a boy who looked to be about five or six years old. Unlike the others, he was wide awake and clinging to a stuffed toy rabbit. Rhydian kept his voice gentle as he asked, "What's your name, little one?"

The boy clutched his rabbit tighter. Careful not to show how the action tugged at his heart, he tried again. "My name's Rhydian, and despite the scary scars on my face, I only want to help you find your parents. Will you tell me your name?"

The boy closed his eyes. "My parents are gone."

He may not have a name, but the boy spoke with an Irish accent, which told Rhydian he was a long way from home.

"If you tell me what happened, I can try to find them."

The boy shook his head vehemently. "They wouldn't

wake up. I tried and tried. The scary humans said they were dead. Mr. Cottontail is my only family now."

Anger flared and only through years of practice did Rhydian manage to keep it from showing on his face. "You're safe here, boy. I promise you that." Rhydian put out a hand. "Will you give me your hand? I want the doctor to take a look at you."

Opening his eyes, the boy replied, "Will you be there?"

"I will. What's your name, little one?"

"Rian."

"Well, Rian, if you come with me and let the doctor check you out, then I'm sure we can find you some sweets."

"I'm not allowed to have sweets unless it's a special day."

He smiled. "We'll make an exception." He wiggled his fingers. "Give me your hand, Rian."

The boy gingerly placed his hand in his. Rhydian helped the boy to his feet and gently lifted him out. With the child in his arms, he made his way toward Maelon.

His dragon spoke up. *He must be a dragon-shifter since he's unfazed by the ride here.*

Yes, but what is an Irish lad doing in the hands of Welsh dragon hunters?

I have no idea. But we'll ferret it out.

You aren't suggesting we take care of him, I hope.

Why not? He needs protection and has warmed up to us. Moving him again might upset or traumatize him.

Before Rhydian could lay out all the reasons why he didn't have time to look after a child, Rian said, "Your eyes flash like Daddy's."

Rhydian kept his tone light, so as to not frighten the boy. "And your mum's too?"

"No. Mam said she couldn't change into a dragon. Although I wished on my last birthday she could." He looked down at his stuffed toy. "But she never will now."

The boy's eyes grew wet. Rhydian quickly said, "There are lots of dragons here. If you behave for the doctor, you can pet as many as you want."

"Can I? I've only ever seen Daddy's red dragon. But he told me stories of blue and green and gold ones. I want to be a gold dragon. Like a king."

If the boy had only seen his father shift into a dragon, it probably meant the boy's father had fallen for a human and had gone into hiding to be with her since Ireland rarely allowed humans to live with the dragon clans.

And with the recent turmoil in Ireland over the death of two clan leaders and the ensuing battles for power and control over those two clans, Rian's parent had probably fled to Wales for safety until things calmed down back home.

But he could think on all of that later. For the moment, he smiled at Rian. "Then let's hurry up and get you checked out. How about you tell me about Mr. Cottontail on the way?"

As the boy explained the history of his stuffed toy rabbit, Rhydian walked briskly toward the surgery. The others should already be there. Once he had Rian examined, he could check on Delia and the other children.

And while he still had a lot of work ahead of him with regards to cleaning up his clan and enforcing the rules properly, he now had another reason beyond his own past to fight for human acceptance within his clan. Rian's parents weren't the only ones who'd had to go into hiding in order to be with the person they loved. He knew a few of his own clan members who had done the same over the years.

It may have been the wrong time for change all those years ago, when he'd fought for his human lover, but he'd make sure now was the right one.

For as long as Rhydian remained leader, he'd ensure his clan's policy on humans shifted. Going forward, he wanted his clan members to mate for love, regardless if their mate could change into a dragon or not.

CHAPTER NINE

Staring down at his sister's unconscious form, Kai did his best to contain his desire to seek out those responsible and make them pay for harming a mere child.

His dragon chimed in. *While I agree, the doctor needs our attention right now. It's the best way to help Delia.*

It took everything he had to focus on Dr. Perry's words. "We don't know if there will be any long-term effects from the drugs we found in her system. We've managed to flush out as much as we could. However, the good news is that all of her vital signs are normal now. She'll pull through."

Kai looked at the doctor. "How long until the results come back from the tests being run on the drugs?"

Dr. Perry answered, "Thanks to Trahern's assistance on Stonefire, we should hopefully have them by tomorrow."

Kai's mother cleared her throat and touched the tender, pink skin that outlined Delia's tattoo that had once been on her upper arm but was no longer there. "I don't care if it's the middle of the night, you call me the instant you know what's going on, Maelon."

"Of course, Lily," Dr. Perry replied. "I'll also make sure that a nurse brings you a cot and blankets since I know you'll be staying here until your daughter wakes up."

Kai's mother bobbed her head and took Delia's hand in hers.

At the sight of his mother and sister, the urge to punch the bastards responsible coursed through his body. Since the DDA now had the few humans Snowridge's Protectors had captured at the farm—the three men from Arabella's images plus a few others—in custody, seeing any of them was nigh impossible. All he could do was continue to assist Snowridge in piecing together the facts to find out what exactly had happened back on that farm.

In order to do that, he needed more information on what the doctor had discovered so far.

Looking at the doctor, Kai motioned with his head toward the hallway. Once they were both there and the door to Delia's room was closed, Kai stated, "Tell me everything that you know, even if it's only conjecture at this point." When Maelon Perry hesitated, Kai added, "Rhydian already gave me the highest clearance regarding this matter. But I can't do anything if people keep secrets from me."

After checking that the hallway was empty, Maelon spoke in a low voice. "All of the children had the same drugs in their systems, according to preliminary tests. The kidnapped farmers' children had higher toxicity levels, which means they've been exposed longer and I have no idea what effect that will have on them."

If it was anything like the attacks on Stonefire, their inner dragons might go rogue.

His dragon spoke up. *What about those too young to talk with their dragons yet?*

Dragon-shifters usually started talking with their inner beasts around age six or seven. *I don't know. Let's hope their dragons still emerge when they should.*

Yes, otherwise that'll be lonely for them.

Worse than that, dragon-shifters without inner dragons usually went insane .

Maelon's voice interrupted Kai's thoughts. "There is

one positive so far, though. The only half-human and half dragon-shifter child had the same drugs in his system, but the boy appears unaffected."

"Does that mean the drugs only affect pure-blooded dragon-shifters?"

"It's too early to make a definitive statement, but it seems so. Or, at least, it works on dragon-shifters who only have a tiny percentage of human ancestry. Very few of us are genetically 100 percent dragon-shifter."

Kai grunted. "Right, then maybe you should figure out at what point the drug becomes ineffective. That way we know who is at higher risk and then can decide who needs the most protection in future battles or attacks."

Raising his brows, Maelon said, "I'm going to pretend that you didn't just imply I'm not doing my job. We're already working on it."

His dragon spoke up. *Be nice to the doctor. He's helping Jane.*

Kai was about to apologize for his curt tone when one of the male nurses rushed up to them. "Kai, your mate's finally awake."

Jane. Without a word, Kai raced down the hall to his mate's room. He threw open the door to find Jane sitting up in her bed, frowning down at a bowl of soup.

Closing the distance between them, he stopped next to her bed and cupped her cheek. "Janey."

She smiled up at him. "Hello there."

He leaned down and gave her a gentle kiss. "I'm so sorry, love."

Raising her brows, she slowly turned her upper body toward him, grunting as she did it. "What the hell are you apologizing for?"

"Kissing Maggie, for a start. Then there's the fact that you're injured and it's all my fault."

She tilted her head. "I'll admit that I wanted to punch Maggie when you kissed her, but I understand why you did it. I might not be here to forgive you if not for that bloody kiss."

"Jane, I—"

"Just stop, Kai. The only person at fault here is Maggie and her warped view of the world. To be honest, I'm just happy her kiss didn't start a mate-claim frenzy. Care to explain that to a lowly human?" He growled and she smiled. "Okay, care to explain it to a brilliant, amazing human such as myself?"

His dragon spoke up. *Her humor means that she's okay.*

Ignoring his beast, he replied, "It's simple—I didn't want her."

"And?"

"Too much time had passed. All I need or want is you, Jane Hartley."

"I hope that also means you know I'm going to stick around. If I can suffer someone piercing me with a talon and still love you, that's saying something."

He blinked. "Surely it can't be that easy."

"Why not? You're the most honorable male I know. Although if you lord that over my brother, so help me, I will retaliate."

He grinned. "Thanks for the idea."

She rolled her eyes. "Speaking of Rafe, does he know what happened?"

"Yes. He was torn between staying with Nikki and seeing you. I told him to stay on Stonefire and that you'd do a video conference as soon as you're strong enough."

"I'd say I'm feeling well considering everything, but let's not tell Rafe that just yet. I need to conserve my energy for that conversation."

"If he upsets you, I will challenge him the next time I see him."

She let out a breath. "Don't waste time thinking about that. Just stay with me a while and fill me in on what happened. The nurse mentioned something about Delia being back, but then he left before I could ask anything."

He pointed to the soup. "Only if you allow me to feed you some of that."

She wrinkled her nose. "You know how much I hate soup. A meal shouldn't be a liquid."

Pulling a chair next to Jane's bed, he sat down. "You'll eat it or I won't share any information."

She clicked her tongue. "You know, if I were anyone else, I'd play on your guilt to get the information."

He picked up the spoon and scooped up some soup. "But you aren't and you won't. Now, open up."

With a sigh, she complied and choked down some soup. Kai merely shook his head. "And you say I'm a baby when I'm injured." She opened her mouth to reply, but he beat her to it. "But enough of that. Let me tell you everything I know."

As Kai explained about Delia, the children, the drugs, and Maelon Perry's findings, Kai slowly forced Jane to eat her soup. When he finished the recap, he added, "And there's one more thing I'm not sure anyone on Snowridge knows about."

Curiosity danced in her eyes. "Oh? Do tell. I'd lean in close, but my shoulder bloody hurts, even with all the meds they have me on."

A flare of concern flashed, but he pushed it away. The best medicine for Jane was to keep her brain active. The second he started to hide things, she'd get the crazy idea to get out of bed and start hunting for information on her own.

"Well, the drugs and Delia's missing tattoo remind me of what happened to Killian O'Shea. They found him with no memory of his past life, his dragon, and he also had his tattoo lasered off."

"Is Delia the same way?"

"I don't know. The one difference is that the doctors were able to flush her system. We won't know anything until she wakes up."

"Oh, Kai. I have faith that she'll wake up with her memory intact. Stubbornness does run in the blood, after all."

He took her hand. "I hope so."

She gently squeezed his fingers. "I can tell you're anxious to do something to help. I can manage here, Kai. Go and help Snowridge's Protectors."

"I can't. There's something else you don't know." Kai explained about the corruption and Rhydian cleaning house before adding, "Sebastian and Zain are here already, helping them. Protecting you is my top priority, Janey. I'm not going anywhere."

Jane tried to hide her yawn, but failed. He added, "You need to sleep, love."

"I would argue, but I can barely keep my eyes open. Being stabbed really takes its toll on a person."

"I know," he stated matter-of-factly.

"Oh? There's a story I don't know about. It can't be worse than when you were shot."

He smiled. "Sleep and I'll tell you when you wake up—after a reasonable amount of time. No twenty-minute naps allowed."

"My, someone's bossy."

He released her hand and crossed his arms over his chest. "I will channel Nurse Ginny if I have to."

Ginny was the toughest nurse on Stonefire and handled all the most alpha patients.

Jane sighed. "As much as I'd like to see you wear a wig and put on a nurse's outfit, even I will admit I need the sleep. Give me a gentle dragon cuddle and I'll comply."

His dragon spoke up. *Yes, lots of dragon cuddles.*

Kai ignored his beast to hug Jane as gently as he could, all while pressing his cheek to hers. "I love you, Janey."

"I love you, too, Kai."

After releasing his mate, he lightly traced her cheek. "Sweet dreams, love. The faster you heal, the faster I can take you home."

Jane slowly laid down. "Not until Delia's well."

He was about to argue, but Jane's eyes slid closed and she was out within seconds.

His beast said, *I knew Jane would forgive us.*

Kai grunted. *I still wonder how I deserve her.*

Maybe you don't, but I do, his dragon teased.

Mentally giving his beast the double finger salute, Kai then watched the rise and fall of Jane's chest. One part of his world looked to remain intact, but the question was whether his sister would fair the same way or not.

⚬⚬⚬⚬⚬

Rhydian Griffiths stared at Rian on the sofa in his office, fast asleep. The boy had lasted only a few minutes after eating his meal before passing out.

With his arms sprawled wide and his mouth open, it was hard to believe the boy had suffered so much recently. Although judging by his lack of hysterics, Rhydian had a feeling the boy didn't truly understand that his parents weren't coming back.

His dragon spoke up. *We will look after him.*

Only until I can find a relative. The boy mentioned his human aunt a few times. She may be his best chance at a

93

normal life with someone who wants him.

I want him.

He's not a pet that we can keep, dragon. Rian deserves someone who understands children and can raise him. I, on the other hand, can barely keep this clan together.

That's only because you ignored my suggestions. The old ways are fading. We need to be like Stonefire.

He hated to admit that the bloody English dragon clan was leading the way with change. *More like we need to be like the Welsh clans of old, when they helped lead the way among dragon-shifters in this region of the world.*

Until the humans known as the Normans came and hunted us.

Both human and dragon-shifter had been hit hard by the Norman Conquest and ensuing castle-slash-fortification building that began in Wales during the 11th century. *Unless the dragon hunters become more organized and formidable, we don't have to worry about anyone else conquering our country.* Rian rolled over in his sleep, garnering Rhydian's attention once more. *All that matters is creating a better future for the children. Now, let me get to work.*

His beast retreated to the back of his mind.

Rhydian sat at his desk and brought up his video conference program. Trahern Lewis was due to call with an update in the next few minutes, regarding any new information about the drugs used on Delia and the others. While he had a feeling Trahern's report wasn't going to be good, Rhydian wasn't about to worry more than he had to. Besides, worry was a distraction he couldn't afford at the moment.

Rhydian eyed the stack of papers that his trusted Protector Wren had given him. Each packet represented a Protector who Wren believed wasn't as loyal to Snowridge as they were to themselves. Replacing them was going to be difficult since each Protector needed two years with the British Army before joining the Protector ranks, according to formal agreements made with the Department of Dragon Affairs.

He wished there was a way to streamline the process, but even Rhydian understood the value of time spent in the army. Not only for the chance to work with and understand humans, but to also learn tactics the Snowridge Protectors might not know about.

He might just have to take up Bram's offer to loan him a few of his Protectors for a while, and maybe take on a few from the Scottish clan as well.

If Rhydian had been looking for change, inviting the English and Scottish dragons to live with his clan definitely fit the bill.

But before he did that, he would find Rian's aunt and finish his draft of the new clan charter. The rules would no longer be vague regarding humans and other clans. It was time to open his clan's eyes to more of the world. Their remote location would no longer protect them in the ever-shrinking technological world.

Just as he began reading the first possible trouble-maker's file, his video conference application chimed. He quickly hit Receive and Trahern's brown-eyed, black-haired form came online. Having known the male since he was a baby, Rhydian dispensed with formalities. "What new information do you have?"

Trahern didn't hesitate with his reply. "We're still waiting on a few test results, but I'm almost positive that the formula you provided is nearly a match for what was found in Killian O'Shea's body."

"But not the same as what was used on Dr. Sid and others on Stonefire?"

"It's not a completely different composition, but more elements match Killian's case. I should have the exact chemical make up of the samples tomorrow."

"While I appreciate your quick work on this, Trahern, I'm hoping you have something that can help the children who were targeted and pumped full of these drugs."

"Until I have the exact chemical makeup, I'm uncomfortable suggesting anything."

Rhydian growled, "Doctor Davies, if you're there, speak up."

The slightly plump face of Dr. Emily Davies came on screen. While she had never been welcome on Snowridge in the past, Rhydian had become familiar with the Welsh human's work on Stonefire recently. She said, "Trahern's right to wait for the results."

"I sense a 'but,' Doctor Davies."

To her credit, the human took her time adjusting her glasses before saying anything. It seemed she'd grown accustomed to dragon-shifter dominance. "The moss we used here on Dr. Sid and the others can't hurt. Even if it's ineffective against the new compound, it's harmless to all dragon-shifters."

"What about half dragon-shifters?"

Dr. Davies leaned forward. "There was a half-human child? Why did no one mention this?" She looked to Trahern. "Did you know about this?"

"I only know what was in the records," Trahern stated off-screen. "The full results tomorrow will reveal their genetics."

Dr. Davies rolled her eyes. "Trahern, I wonder about you sometimes."

Sensing the pair would keep chatting about the small detail, Rhydian barked, "Anything else? Otherwise, I need to attend to my clan."

Dr. Davies sat up taller. "That's all for now. We'll let you know when the results are in."

The screen went blank before Rhydian could so much as open his mouth.

Still, despite the human's backbone and behavior, Rhydian's desire to change his clan's policy on humans didn't waver. If anything, he appreciated her tendency to speak her mind. It was a hell of a lot easier than dealing with Trahern's long, detailed conversations.

A groan came from the direction of the sofa. Rhydian noticed the boy frowning in his sleep and turning his head this way and that.

It was then that Rhydian noticed the toy rabbit on the floor. Rushing to the boy's prized Mr. Cottontail, he snatched it up and pressed it against Rian's chest. He instantly hugged the toy and his movements calmed down.

He hesitated a second before brushing the hair off Rian's forehead. The boy wouldn't stay on Snowridge forever, but as long as he did, he would drive Rhydian to work harder.

Moving to his desk, he began sorting through his paperwork. The sooner he cleaned house, the sooner he could put his clan on the path to a better future.

CHAPTER TEN

$\mathcal{A}$ few days later, Jane leaned against Kai as they made their way down the hall to Delia's room. "I wish they would've told us more than simply saying that Delia is awake."

"Would you have preferred me arguing on the phone instead of just making our way to her room ourselves?" Kai asked.

"No. I just, well, no matter what anyone says, I still feel a little bit responsible."

"I would argue, but I don't think you'll listen."

She frowned. "What happened to being nice to me?"

The corner of Kai's mouth ticked up. "You're the one who wanted me to stop treating you as if you'd break. Besides, the doctor said you're healing nicely. The shot of my blood really sped up your healing process."

"I would say thank you, but for a while you kept trying to make me sign a sacrifice contract."

Kai grinned. "I couldn't resist, although my version of the contract was slightly different. I didn't require pregnancy, just lots of sex once you're healed."

She rolled her eyes. "Lots of kinky sex, I should add."

They approached the door. "Unless you want to talk about all the sex acts I put into writing in front of my mother and stepfather, you might want to drop it for now."

Jane stuck out her tongue before whispering, "This conversation isn't finished."

Kai winked, and Jane couldn't help but smile. She took each and every moment as a gift. Kai had kissed his once-true mate and hadn't wanted her.

More than that, he hadn't even joked about requiring a baby in exchange for his blood.

Jane was enough for him.

Between that and the positive responses she'd seen for her first video episode, Jane only hoped Delia was okay. If so, it would make her day almost perfect.

They entered the hospital room to find Delia sitting upright in her bed with Lily and Gareth on one side, and Rhydian and Dr. Perry on the other.

Delia's green eyes met hers and Jane held her breath.

As soon as the teenager smiled, Jane relaxed a fraction. Delia said, "You two are here. Now I can give my big report."

Closing the distance to Delia's bed, Kai asked, "What report?"

Rhydian answered, "The one where she tells us what she found out."

Jane put up a hand. "Wait, first tell us if Delia remembers everything."

Delia opened her mouth, but Dr. Perry beat her to it. "For the most part. Her dragon is a bit groggy but responsive. We won't be able to fully assess the damage until she shifts into a dragon."

Rhydian grunted. "Yes, yes, now tell us what you know, Delia Owens. I'm done being patient."

At the steel in his voice, Delia didn't hesitate to answer. "Using my investigative skills, I located a splinter dragon hunter group on that farm. There's no gang in this part of Wales, so they came from somewhere down south. However, that's not the important bit."

She paused and Lily spoke up. "Now is not the time for your dramatics, Delia. Just tell us everything, and quickly."

Delia nodded. "Right, well, once I found the farm and poked around, I knew I wouldn't be able to truly understand what was happening unless I got caught. So, I staged a dramatic scene, complete with screaming and acting scared."

"Bloody fool," Kai muttered under his breath.

Jane ignored him to focus on Delia's story. The teenager continued, "It worked, brother. At any rate, they put me in a cage with all the other children. In addition to the farmers' kids, there was the Irish boy."

"Rian's safe," Rhydian stated.

Delia nodded. "As I suspected would be the case, the humans didn't take care of what they said in front of me or the children. They talked about purchase orders streaming in for their silent dragon drug, as well as a successful test done in Ireland recently. They didn't say who, but just that it was a male."

Jane shared a glance with Kai. She had to be talking about Killian.

The young dragon-shifter continued, "Their plan was to test the same drug on me, the only one with an active dragon. I was an unplanned trial, I think. The children were the main focus and were to be long-term tests, to see if preventing their dragons from ever speaking to their human halves made their prisoners more malleable."

Even Jane knew that inner dragons usually didn't speak up until a child reached six or seven years old. After mating and living with Kai, she also knew how important an inner dragon was to their human half. To think the poor children might never know their constant inner companion and integral part of their personality caused Jane's heart to drop.

Delia shuddered and Lily placed a hand on her daughter's shoulder. The touch gave Delia the strength to carry on. "Watching them give the little ones shot after shot was hard to stand. I wanted to shift and free them, but the humans must've given me something to temporarily prevent me from shifting because I couldn't do it. The restraints were also strong enough to keep me from kicking their arses."

Kai and Lily both opened their mouths to most likely scold Delia, but Dr. Perry spoke first. "The children are all alive, Delia, and most likely thanks to you going after them. I think that's all that matters."

Lily muttered, "Don't encourage her."

Delia met the doctor's eyes. "You have to say it'll be okay since you're my doctor. But the children might not have their dragons when they're older. That's an unfair punishment for any dragon-shifter, but more so for an innocent child."

Kai growled. "We'll stop these bastards, no matter what. Seizing their farm and their chemicals was a good first step, and all thanks to you. I still think you're a fool for going on your own, but you helped the children we rescued, Delia. That kept them from a long-term imprisonment that would eventually lead to them being blood slaves. Remember that."

Jane wanted to reassure the girl, but Rhydian grunted and placed his hand on Delia's shoulder. "I concur about the stupidity of going out alone, but you did a good job, Delia. Next time, come to me first. Then we can try to rescue or help who needs it without giving your mother and father extra gray hairs from worry."

Delia looked to her parents. Despite the girl's actions,

she was still just a teenager who wanted to hug her mum and dad.

Jane jumped in. "I think all of this is a bit overwhelming. Let's give Lily and Gareth some time alone with their daughter." She met Rhydian's eyes and didn't flinch at his stare. "She can give a more coherent report after some more rest, don't you think?"

After holding Jane's gaze another beat, Rhydian looked to Lily and Gareth. "Let me know when Delia's rested enough to give her official report." As soon as Lily bobbed her head, he moved his gaze to Kai and Jane. "You two and I need to talk. Let's take Jane back to her room and do it there."

She was tempted to argue, but while she was healing, Jane was still exhausted from her recent ordeal and would love nothing more than to sit down again. "Then what are we waiting for?"

Kai glanced down at her. "That was easy."

She gave an imperceptible shake of her head, signaling not now.

Kai must've caught her meaning because he leaned down to kiss his sister's cheek. Once upright again, he said, "Let me know if you need anything, Mum."

Lily made a shooing motion with her hands. "Yes, yes, now go before your mate falls over."

Jane turned toward the door and Kai took the hint. As they exited the room and made their way down the hall again, Jane wondered what Rhydian wanted to discuss with them.

⁓⁓⁓⁓

Kai made sure Jane was sitting on the arm chair in the corner of her hospital room before he faced Rhydian and waited.

The Welsh leader could play dominance games if he wanted. But instead, he merely started talking. "I need your help."

He blinked. "What?"

"I wouldn't ask if it weren't absolutely necessary. However, Stonefire has far more people currently serving with the British Army than we do, which means you should have an influx of Protectors soon enough."

"Perhaps. But isn't this something you should discuss with my clan leader?"

"I already did, but Bram said I needed your permission for anything Protector-related."

His dragon spoke up. *As it should be.*

Hush. Kai focused back on Rhydian. "What *exactly* are you asking for? I need numbers, specifics, and reasons why you need them before I can make any sort of important decision."

"I'm almost done sorting through my clan and figuring out who's a threat or not. If my initial instincts are correct, I'll be down ten Protectors. Wren and Eira can manage in the short-term with your blokes, Zain and Sebastian, but only for so long. While we're lucky to be more isolated than other dragon clans in the UK, I expect for there to be some retaliation for our dismantling the dragon drug operation near Dolgellau. I need skilled and trustworthy Protectors to help keep Snowridge safe, when and if that happens."

Kai studied the Snowridge leader. Admitting faults and possible shortcomings was never easy, but less so for a clan leader.

His dragon chimed in. *I also believe the sincerity in his voice. We should help him.*

If you gave me a bloody second, you'd know I feel the

same way.

But?

But there will be conditions.

Kai finally spoke aloud. "I'll need to document all potential new Protectors finishing their army stints and assess their skills. But as long as you formalize your alliance with Stonefire and keep an open line of communication, I'm more than willing to assist you."

"Just like that?" Rhydian asked skeptically.

"Bram will contact you with the final alliance details. I already know you're supposed to trade foster candidates soon. I'm sure there'll be more conditions, including one more of my own."

Rhydian searched his gaze. "I hope you don't plan on adding more and more conditions. As much as I need help, I'm not about to be jerked around on a lead for the rest of my life."

Kai shook his head. "Nor do I plan to do that. But I think it's more than time for my mate's family to come visit my mother. I want you to work with the DDA to secure a visit for Jane's parents. If her brother doesn't piss me off, he'll already have clearance since he's a member of Stonefire. Jane's parents, on the other hand, will need protection and formal permission."

Jane took his hand in hers and squeezed. He returned the gesture but never took his gaze from Rhydian's.

Rhydian finally spoke up. "I'll only agree to that condition once I'm sure the clan is safe for them, and not before."

"I wouldn't expect anything else," Kai stated.

Rhydian put out his hand. "Then we have a deal."

Taking the leader's hand, he shook it. "Unless there's anything else that can't wait, my mate needs to rest. We can talk more later."

When Jane didn't protest, Kai knew he'd judged her drooping eyelids correctly.

Releasing his grip, Rhydian nodded and moved to the door. "Keep your phone on, just in case. I'll contact you later."

The instant the door closed behind Snowridge's leader, Kai leaned down and gently lifted Jane into his arms.

She sighed. "I should protest and say I can walk, but I'm more tired than I'd like to admit."

He carried her to the bed and gently laid her down. Once he was laying next to her, she moved to rest her head on his chest, careful to not bang her still-healing shoulder.

Kai wrapped his arm around his mate and said, "Dragon's blood speeds up the healing process, but isn't an instant cure. Rest, Janey. I'll stay awake and watch over you."

She snuggled into his chest. "Keep this up and I might agree to some suggestions in your fake sacrifice contract."

"Oh? Which ones?"

Smiling, she said, "It'll be a surprise. I know how much you hate them, but in this instance, I think you'll like it."

He kissed the top of Jane's head. "When it comes to you, Jane, I'll love anything and everything you do."

She yawned. "Careful, dragonman. That may come back to bite you in the arse."

"As long as you're doing the biting, I'm fine with it."

Her chuckled turned into a groan. "Don't make me laugh, Kai. It hurts in this position."

"Sorry, Janey. I should probably let you rest alone in the bed. I can watch you from the chair."

She tightened her arm around him. "Don't even think of leaving this bed, Kai. I need my big hunk of dragonman meat by my side. I have trouble sleeping when you're not next to me."

His dragon spoke up. *As it should be. She is our mate. We will always be together.*

Kai agreed with his beast but focused on Jane. "Then your hunk of man meat will be here. Now, rest. The sooner you heal, the sooner you can surprise me."

"Such a male," she mumbled.

After a few beats of silence, he glanced down. Looking at Jane's sleeping face, contentment settled over him.

His sister might still have a long road of recovery and there was much to do before being able to send Protectors to Snowridge, but as long as he had Jane at his side, he could do anything.

She was his mate, end of story. Their life together had barely begun, and he looked forward to every second to come.

Epilogue

Eight Weeks Later

*J*ane paced from one side of the room to the other. "Why are they taking so long to get here?"

Kai's voice filled his mother's living room. "You know Nikki's too pregnant to shift and fly, so they're driving. It takes longer."

She turned on her mate. "I still say you should've gone to get them."

He raised his brows. "A dragon landing in your parents' small village would've caused a stir, not to mention a considerable amount of paperwork to garner permission for me to do so." He patted the empty spot next to him on the sofa. "Come sit down, Janey. Otherwise you'll wear yourself out before your parents arrive."

"I told you that I'm fine. My shoulder is a bit stiff still, but your magical dragon's blood did its job."

Kai shrugged. "They're your parents. But if you end up needing to take a nap or pass out from exhaustion, then you get to explain why."

"So much for being a supportive mate."

"I am, but you're being irrational. The meeting will go fine."

"Provided you and Rafe don't kill each other," Jane

muttered.

"I promised to behave and I mean it. Now, come here, Janey."

Jane could fight it and pass the time by arguing with Kai, but her shoulder ached a little from all of the arm swinging she'd done while pacing. With a sigh, she plopped down next to her mate and leaned against him.

Between her videocast series and its PR, following the case and prison sentence against Maggie Jones, and working on her own recovery, Jane hadn't had a lot of downtime with her mate. Kai had been busy as well with finalizing agreements with Snowridge and even helping out Glenlough in Ireland.

Add in the visits to Snowridge to visit Kai's family and help Delia learn to control her dragon once more, and sometimes Jane wondered how she remembered to breathe.

It would be a few weeks yet before they finally could go back to their normal routine, so Jane merely soaked in her dragonman's heat and the sense of comfort that always came with being near him.

Kai spoke up. "I know part of your restlessness is because you're worried about my sister, but she's nearly back to her old self."

Delia's dragon had barely spoken to her at first and had acted more like a young child than a teenager. But with intensive training from Kai, Rhydian, Snowridge's tracker, Carys, and other alpha dragon-shifters, Delia's dragon was learning and maturing. Everyone was hopeful for the future.

Well, at least for Delia's.

"Your sister might be nearly back to normal, but we won't know for years about the other children."

Squeezing her good shoulder, Kai answered, "With all

of Stonefire's doctors working on a cure, they'll find something. I know they will."

"I hope so."

A comfortable silence fell. Jane's eyes grew heavy, but just as she struggled to keep them open, her mother's familiar Australian accent boomed from the entrance. "Jane Elizabeth Hartley, come give your mother a hug."

She looked up to see the tall, red-haired figure of her mother, Leonie Hartley. "Hi, Mum."

When Jane didn't get up, her mother closed the distance and scrutinized her face. "Should you even be socializing yet? You had a nasty injury not that long ago and look tired." She glanced at Kai. "Are you going to back me up on this, Kai?"

Jane put up a hand. "Just stop, please, Mother. Today isn't about my health." She stood and hugged her mum. "Where are the others? And Dad?"

"Your father is with Rafe and Nikki. Something about Rafe wanting to make sure Nikki doesn't fall down the stairs."

Jane rolled her eyes. "She might be six months pregnant, but she's not that big yet."

"You know your brother and how protective he is of those he cares for. He could have twenty people telling him Nikki was fine and he'd remain skeptical." Leonie placed a hand on her hip and stared at Kai. "Where're your parents?"

Kai looked over at the door leading to the kitchen. "They should've heard you come in."

Jane wondered if Kai was referencing her mother's tendency to talk loudly, but managed not to smile. She merely patted Kai's arm. "Go get them. The more people in the room when Rafe arrives, the better. You'll both behave more."

Grunting, Kai glared at her. "I can behave. He's the one being irrational. You'd think he had pregnancy hormones racing through his body instead of Nikki."

Snorting, Jane opened her mouth to reply when her mother cut her off. "Of course you can behave, dear. But I'd like to meet your mother. We did just drive more hours than I'd like just to get here."

Sighing, Jane resisted placing her face in her hands. She loved her mother, but sometimes she was a bit over the top. "Please don't guilt trip him this early in the visit, Mum."

Her mum tsked. "I'm just being honest. If you don't know that my nature is to speak the truth by now, then I don't know how you ever made a living as a journalist."

Jane was tempted to rub her forehead. "How about maybe toning it down just a bit? At least until after I can introduce you to Kai's family? I don't want them running for the hills before that. Speaking of which, maybe that's why they're hiding."

"Jane Hartley, I appreciate some backbone, but I expect a little respect from my favorite daughter."

"I'm your only daughter."

Her mum waved a hand. "That doesn't matter. And this is who I am, so if it embarrasses you, I'll leave."

Kai chuckled. "Please don't, Leonie. You and Jane are more alike than I think my mate wants to acknowledge."

Jane was about to protest, but Lily and Gareth entered the room, with Delia right behind him. Jane jumped at the distraction. "Mum, this is Kai's mum and stepdad, Lily and Gareth. The younger one is his sister, Delia. Everyone, this is my mum, Leonie Hartley."

Lily rushed to Jane's mum and smiled. "Nice to finally meet you, Leonie. It'll be nice to trade stories with another parent of a stubborn child."

"Tell me about it. Jane made not eating her lunches into an art form."

"Mum, please," Jane said.

Lily replied as if Jane hadn't spoken. "Kai was the same with baths as a toddler. I half expected potatoes to start growing out of his ears."

Jane glanced at Kai and he shrugged. "I don't remember it."

She opened her mouth to ask for details, but Nikki's voice boomed into the room. "Stop it, Rafe. I mean it. Ask me again if I'm okay and I swear I'll cut off one of your balls tonight."

"You're the one huffing up the stairs. Me asking about your health is to be expected," Rafe stated.

Her dad's calm voice came next. "Son, I'd leave it be if I were you. I think she's serious."

Nikki replied, "Of course I am. And thank you, Tom, for noticing when I need a break."

"That isn't fair, Nikki," Rafe replied. "I'm allowed to be protective when your health is concerned, per our agreement."

"I think maybe we should revisit that agreement, to include you need to leave me be when you're being a pain in my arse."

Her dad's stern voice interjected, "I think this argument can wait. Otherwise, we may never be invited back here."

Rafe and Nikki murmured their apologies.

Kai whispered, "Your dad may not be a dragon-shifter, but he knows how to put dominance in his voice."

Jane looked askance at her mate. "Do you blame him? He had to live with the three of us."

Kai grinned. "Fair point."

Nikki, Rafe, and her dad came into the room. Her dad's tall, gray-haired form walked between Nikki and Rafe, no doubt to act as a buffer. He'd done the same thing many times in the past to keep Jane and Rafe from killing each other as children.

Jane stood and Kai followed suit. Jane motioned toward her dad. "Everyone, this is my dad, Tom Hartley." She pointed to each member of Kai's family in turn and introduced them. Her dad nodded when she finished.

Lily clapped her hands. "Right, now that everyone is here, let's head into the kitchen and dining room. I have snacks laid out and I'll put the kettle on for some tea."

Rafe muttered, "I need something stronger if you have it."

Nikki shot her mate a glance and then walked toward Jane. Threading her arm through hers, Nikki said, "I think it's time for us to chat a bit, Jane. It seems my presence has driven my mate to drinking."

Sighing, Rafe said, "Nikki, that's not what I meant and you know it."

Jane glanced at Kai and he reluctantly went to Rafe and her father. Kai slapped Rafe's shoulder. "Come, I think there's some larger in the kitchen. My mum might even have a secret stash of whiskey, too."

When Rafe merely nodded, Jane knew her brother was stressed. She leaned to Nikki's ear and whispered, "He might be a pain in your arse, but it's a sign of how much he loves you."

"I know that rationally. But carrying Rafe's spawn is making me irritable and cranky. The next two or three months can't go by fast enough."

Jane drew Nikki's arm closer and squeezed. "Then let's try distracting you. Your second-in-command duties have helped, but once you have some of Lily's cooking, you'll forget about everything else but filling your plate whilst you still can."

Nikki grinned. "I remember from my last visit to Snow-ridge." She tugged on Jane's arm. "Come on. Let's hurry and snap up as much as we can before the males get to it."

Fully on board with the plan, Jane walked into the kitchen and past the males. As she and Nikki loaded up their plates, Jane glanced to Kai standing at the other side of the kitchen. The sight of him and his stepdad drinking beer with her dad and brother made her smile. As much as she loved the passion and love of her relationship with Kai, the little things made it that much dearer.

And for the first time, she didn't doubt that they'd be old and gray one day, making more memories with those that they loved. Kai was her future, and she couldn't wait to see what it held.

Author's Note

Thanks for continuing Kai and Jane's journey. Believe it or not, I see more things in store for them in the future. Some couples have a lot of growing to do, and this pair is definitely one of them!

As an aside, I know that quite a few people wanted Kai and Jane's original story, *Reawakening the Dragon*, to end differently. However, I knew there was a lot more to come with regards to Maggie Jones, so much so that an extra thousand words in an epilogue wouldn't be enough. That's why *Reawakening* ended the way it did—it proved Kai loved Jane and didn't care about Maggie. And yet, there was room to play with all three characters in the future. By now, readers should be used to the fact I continue stories throughout the series, which means a couple is rarely "done and discarded" at the end of their book. If you're reading the tenth book in the Stonefire series, then I hope you trust me by now! :)

Okay, with that out of the way I have some people I need to thank for helping me to get this book out to the world:

- To Becky Johnson and her team at Hot Tree Editing—you all are amazing. Becky gets me and helps my stories shine.
- To Clarissa Yeo of Yocla Designs—you yet again designed a beautiful cover that captures my couple perfectly. I couldn't imagine my series without your magic.

- To Donna H., Alyson S., and Iliana G.—My three betas are amazing and provide valuable honesty. Not only that, they catch the little typos that slip through. All three of you are appreciated more than you know. <3

And as always, I thank you, the reader, for supporting my dragons this long. When I first published *Sacrificed to the Dragon* I had no idea I'd reach double digits with the series, but here we are! Thanks a million times from my heart for not only reading, but also spreading the word. Word-of-mouth is more powerful than you think. And if you want a whole new way to experience my dragons, then maybe check out my audiobooks. There's nothing better than listening to my British narrator and his take on dragon-shifters for hours... ;)

My next release will be *The Heir* (Kelderan Runic Warriors #3), out in January 2018. However, if you're curious about my dragons, *Craved by the Dragon* (Stonefire Dragons #11, about Killian and Brenna), will be out in March 2018.

Thanks so much for reading and I hope to see at the end of the next book! If you haven't read it yet, enjoy a preview of the first Lochguard spinoff book, *The Dragon's Dilemma.*

The Dragon's Dilemma
(Lochguard Highland Dragons #1)

In order to pay for her father's life-saving cancer treatment, Holly Anderson offers herself up as a sacrifice and sells the vial of dragon's blood. In return, she will try to bear a Scottish dragon-shifter a child. While the dragonman assigned to her is kind, Holly can't stop looking at his twin brother. It's going to take everything she has to sleep with her assigned dragonman. If she breaks the sacrifice contract and follows her heart, she'll go to jail and not be able to take care of her father.

Even though he's not ready to settle down, Fraser MacKenzie supports his twin brother's choice to take a female sacrifice to help repopulate the clan. Yet as Fraser gets to know the lass, his dragon starts demanding something he can't have—his brother's sacrifice.

Holly and Fraser fight the pull between them, but one nearly stolen kiss will change everything. Will they risk breaking the law and betraying Fraser's twin? Or, will they find a way out of the sacrifice contract and live their own happily ever after?

Excerpt from *The Dragon's Dilemma*:

CHAPTER ONE

*H*olly Anderson paid the taxi driver and turned toward the large stone and metal gates behind her. Looking up, she saw "Lochguard" spelled out in twisting metal, as well as some words written in a language she couldn't read.

The strange words only reminded her of where she was standing—at the entrance to the Scottish dragon-shifter clan lands.

Taking a deep breath, Holly willed her stomach to settle. She'd signed up for this. In exchange for trying to conceive a dragon-shifter's child, Clan Lochguard had given her a vial of dragon's blood. The money from the sale of that dragon's blood was funding her father's experimental cancer treatments.

All she had to do was spend the next six months sleeping with a dragon-shifter. If she didn't conceive, she could go home. If she did, then she would stay until the baby was born.

What was a minimum of six months of her life if it meant her father could live?

That's if you don't die giving birth to a half-dragon-shifter baby.

Readjusting the grip on her suitcase, Holly pushed aside

the possibility. From everything she'd read, great scientific strides were being made when it came to the role dragon hormones played on a human's body. If she were lucky, there might even be a way to prevent her from dying in nine to fifteen months' time, depending on the date of conception.

This isn't work. Stop thinking about conception dates and birthing babies. After all, she might luck out and never conceive at all.

Holly moved toward the front entrance and took in the view of the loch off to the side. The dull color of the lake's surface was calm, with rugged hills and mountains framing it. Considering she was in the Scottish Highlands in November, she was just grateful that it wasn't raining.

She wondered if it was raining back in Aberdeen.

Thinking of home and her father brought tears to her eyes. He was recovering well from his first course of cancer treatments, but her father's health could decline at any moment. If only dragon's blood could cure cancer, then she wouldn't have to worry.

But since cancer was one of the illnesses dragon's blood couldn't cure, surely the Department of Dragon Affairs would grant her another few weeks to help take care of her father if she asked.

As the taxi backed down the drive, Holly turned around and flagged for the driver to come back. However, before she could barely raise a hand, a voice boomed from the right. "Lass, over here."

She turned toward the voice and a tall, blond man waved her over with a smile.

Between his wind-tousled hair, twinkling eyes, and his grin, the man was gorgeous.

Not only that, he'd distracted her from doing something daft. If Holly ran away before finishing her contract, she'd end up in jail. And then who would take care of her father? The man motioned again. "Come, lass. I won't bite."

When he winked, some of Holly's nervousness faded. Despite the rumors of dragon-shifters being monsters, she'd followed the news stories over the last year and knew Lochguard was one of the good dragon clans. Rumors even said the Lochguard dragons and the local humans had once set up their own sacrifice system long before the British government had implemented one nationwide.

It was time to experience the dragon-shifters firsthand and learn the truth.

Pushing her shoulders back, Holly put on her take no-crap nurse expression and walked over to the dragonman. When she was close enough, she asked, "Who are you?"

The man grinned wider. "I'm glad to see you're not afraid of me, lass. That makes all of this a lot easier."

Before she could stop herself, Holly blurted, "Are you really a dragon-shifter?"

The dragonman laughed. "Aye, I am. I'm the clan leader, in fact. The name's Finn. What's yours?"

The easygoing man didn't match the gruff picture she'd conjured up inside her head over the past few weeks.

Still, dragons liked strength, or so her Department of Dragon Affairs counselor had advised her. Her past decade spent as a maternity nurse would serve her well—if she could handle frantic fathers and mothers during labor, she could handle anything. "You're not a very good clan leader if you don't know my name."

Finn chuckled. "I was trying to be polite, Holly." He lowered his voice to a whisper. "Some say we're monsters that eat bairns for breakfast. I was just trying to assure you we can be friendly."

Confident the smiling man wouldn't hurt her for questioning him, she stated, "You could be acting."

"I think my mate is going to like you."

At the mention of the word "mate," Holly's confidence slipped a fraction. After all, she'd soon be having sex with a dragon-shifter to try to conceive a child. That was the price all sacrifices had to pay.

And there was always a small chance she turned out to be the dragon-shifter's true mate. If that happened, she might never be able to see her father again. Dragons were notoriously possessive. She didn't think they'd let a mate go once they found one.

Finn's voice interrupted her thoughts. "Let me take that suitcase, Holly. The sooner we get you to my place, the sooner we can settle you in and answer some of your questions."

Finn put out a hand and she passed the case over. She murmured, "Thank you."

"Considering that you're helping my clan more than you know, the least I can do is carry a bag."

She eyed the tall dragonman. "You don't have to comfort me. I know what I volunteered to do."

Finn raised a blond eyebrow. "You looked about ready to bolt or cry a few minutes ago. I think a little kindness wouldn't hurt."

He was right, not that she would admit to it. After all, she was supposed to be strong.

Holly motioned toward the gates. "How about we go so you can give me the spiel and then let me meet my dragonman?"

The dragonman's smile faded. "So you're giving orders to me now, aye?"

Even though Holly was human, she still sensed the dominance and strength in his voice. She could apologize and try to hide her true self, but that would be too tiring to keep up long term. Instead, she tilted her head. "I'm used to giving orders. In my experience, as soon as a woman goes into labor, her other half goes crazy. If I don't take charge, it could put the mother's life as well as the child's in danger. I'm sure you've read my file and should know what to expect."

The corner of Finn's mouth ticked up. "Aye, I have. But I like to test the waters with potential clan members."

"I'm not—"

Finn cut her off. "Give it time, lass. You may well become one in the long run."

Without another word, Finn started walking. Since he was at least eight inches taller than her, she had to half-jog to catch up to him. However, before she could reply, another tall, muscled dragonman approached. He still had the soft face of late adolescence and couldn't be more than twenty.

The younger dragon-shifter motioned a thumb behind him. "Archie and Cal are at it again. If you don't break it up, they might shift and start dropping each other's cattle for the second time this week."

Finn sighed. "I should assign them a full-time babysitter."

The younger man grinned. "You tried that, but my grandfather escaped, as you'll remember."

"That's because he's a sneaky bastard." Finn looked to Holly. "This is Jamie MacAllister. He'll take you to my mate, Arabella. She can help you get settled before you meet Fergus."

"Who's Fergus?" Holly asked, even though she had a feeling she knew.

Finn answered, "Fergus MacKenzie is my cousin, but he's also your assigned dragonman."

Of course she'd be given the cousin of the clan leader. After all, Holly was the first human sacrifice on Lochguard in over a decade. They'd want to keep tabs on her.

Holly didn't like it, but since she had yet to meet this Fergus, she wouldn't judge him beforehand. For all she knew, Fergus MacKenzie might be a shy, quiet copy of his cousin. Maybe.

Not sure what else to do, Holly nodded. After giving a few more orders, Finn left to address the problem and Jamie smiled down at her. "There's never a dull moment here, lass. Welcome to Lochguard."

Holly wasn't sure if that was a warning or a welcome.

∼◦∼◦∼◦∼

Fraser MacKenzie watched his twin brother from the kitchen. His brother, Fergus, was due to meet his human sacrifice in the next few hours and instead of celebrating his last hours of freedom, Fergus was doing paperwork.

Sometimes, Fraser wondered how they were related at all.

Taking aim, he lobbed an ice cube across the room. It bounced off his brother's cheek and Fraser shouted, "Goal."

Frowning, Fergus glanced over. "Don't you have a hole to dig? Or, maybe, some nails to pound?"

Fraser shrugged a shoulder and inched his fingers toward another ice cube. "I finished work early. After all, it's not every day your twin meets the possible mother of his child."

As Fraser picked up his second ice cube, his mother's voice boomed from behind him. "Put it down, Fraser Moore MacKenzie. I won't have you breaking something if you miss."

He looked at his mother and raised his brows. "I never miss."

Clicking her tongue, his mother, Lorna, moved toward the refrigerator. "Stop lying to me, lad. You missed a step and now have the scar near your eye to prove it."

Fraser resisted the urge to touch his scar. "That was because my sister distracted me." He placed a hand over his heart. "I was just looking out for the wee lass."

Lorna rolled her eyes. "Faye was sixteen at the time and you were too busy glaring at one of the males."

"He was trouble. Faye deserved better," Fraser replied.

Fergus looked up from his paperwork. "Where is Faye?"

Lorna waved a hand. "The same as every day. She leaves early in the morning and I don't see her again until evening."

Fraser sobered up. "I wish she'd let us help her. Does anyone know if she can fly again yet?"

His younger sister, Faye, had been shot out of the sky by an electrical blast nearly two months earlier while in dragon form and her wing had been severely damaged. While she was no longer in a wheelchair, the doctors weren't sure if Faye would ever fly again.

His mother turned toward him. "I trust Arabella to help her. Faye will come to us when she's ready."

Jumping on the chance to lighten the mood again, Fraser tossed the ice cube into the sink and added, "I'm more worried about Fergus right now anyway. Who spends their last few hours of freedom cooped up inside? Even if he doesn't want to go drinking, he could at least go for a flight."

Fergus lifted the papers in his hand. "For your information, this is all of the new procedures and suggestions from the Department of Dragon Affairs. Finn worked hard to make Lochguard one of the trial clans for these new rules, and I'm not about to fuck it up." Lorna clicked her tongue and Fergus added, "Sorry, Mum."

Lorna leaned against the kitchen counter. "I still applaud you for what you're doing, Fergus. After the last fifteen years of near-isolation, the clan desperately needs some new blood."

Fergus shrugged a shoulder. "It's not a guarantee. Besides, how could I pass up the chance to help our cousin?"

Fraser rolled his eyes. "Right, you're being all noble when I know for a fact you just want to, er," he looked to his mum and back to Fergus, "sleep with a human lass."

"No one around here has stirred a mate-claim frenzy and I'm not about to look in the other clans. I'm needed here," Fergus replied. "A human sacrifice is my only other chance."

"And what if she's not your true mate, brother? Then what?" Fraser asked.

"I'll still try to win her over. If she gives me a child, I want to try to convince the human to stay."

Lorna spoke up. "Her father's ill, Fergus. Let's see how things go before you start planning the human's future." Lorna looked to Fraser. "Let's just hope she has spirit. I can handle anything but fear."

Fraser answered, "If Finn picked her out, then we should trust that he chose a good one."

"You're right, son," Lorna answered. She waved toward the living room. "Now, go get that ice cube."

"Fergus is closer. He could just toss it over."

Fergus looked back at his stack of papers. "Get it yourself."

With a sigh, Fraser moved toward the living room. "You were always a lazy sod."

Fergus looked up. "Takes one to know one. But at least this lazy sod is about to get his own cottage."

Lorna's voice drifted into the living room. "It's about time. One down, two more to go."

Fraser scooped up the ice cube and faced his mother. "Don't worry, Mum. You'll always have me. If I'm lucky, I won't have a mate until I'm fifty."

Fergus chimed in. "She'll kick you out on your arse before then."

"I'm feeling the love, brother."

Fergus looked up with a grin. "Someone has to love you, you unlovable bastard."

Tossing the ice cube into the sink, Fraser dried his hands. "You know you'll miss me, Fergus. I give it a week and then you'll be begging for my company."

"We'll see, Fraser. If I'm lucky, I'll be spending a week in my sacrifice's bed."

The thought of not seeing his twin every day did something strange to his heart. Brushing past it, Fraser headed toward the door. "As much as I'd love to stay and watch you read boring protocol, I'm going to watch some paint dry instead."

Fergus raised an auburn eyebrow. "What happened to spending time with your brother?"

"I never said anything about spending time with you. I wanted to show you a good time. The offer's still open if you're interested."

Shaking his head, Fergus answered, "Your good times always result in us waking up in strange places and not remembering the night before. I think I'll stay here."

Fraser shrugged. "Your loss." He looked to his mum. "I'll be home for dinner, don't worry."

Lorna answered. "You'd better be. Finn wants us to have a quiet dinner with Holly and help ease her into her new life here."

"Quiet is a bit of a stretch."

Lorna picked up an apple and tossed it at his head. Once he caught it, she answered, "Just get your arse home on time."

Fraser winked. "I'll try my best, but you know how the lasses love me."

Not wanting to hear his mother's lecture about settling

down for the hundredth time, Fraser ducked out the front door.

While the human wouldn't be over to their house until dinnertime, she was due to arrive on Lochguard at any moment. He had known that Fergus wouldn't want to go out, but asking gave Fraser the perfect cover and no one would suspect what he was about to do.

It was time to spy on his brother's future female and make sure she was worthy of a MacKenzie.

————————————

The Dragon's Dilemma is now available in paperback. Learn more at:

www.jessiedonovan.com

About the Author

Jessie Donovan wrote her first story at age five, and after discovering *The Dragonriders of Pern* series by Anne Mc-Caffrey in junior high, she realized people actually wanted to read stories like those floating around inside her head. From there on out, she was determined to tap into her over-active imagination and write a book someday.

After living abroad for five years and earning degrees in Japanese, Anthropology, and Secondary Education, she buckled down and finally wrote her first full-length book. While that story will never see the light of day, it laid the world-building groundwork of what would become her debut paranormal romance, *Blaze of Secrets*. In late 2014, she became a *New York Times* and *USA Today* bestseller.

Jessie loves to interact with readers, and when not reading or traipsing around some foreign country on a shoestring, she can often be found on Facebook. Check out her pages below:

http://www.facebook.com/JessieDonovanAuthor

And don't forget to sign-up for her newsletter to receive sneak peeks and inside information. You can sign-up on her website:

http:///www.jessiedonovan.com

Made in the USA
Monee, IL
23 August 2022

12189511R00080